D0014817

Geronimo Stilton

Thea Stilton
THE DANCE OF
THE STAR FAIRIES

Scholastic Inc.

Copyright © 2018 by Edizioni Piemme S.p.A., Palazzo Mondadori, Via Mondadori 1, 20090 Segrate, Italy. International Rights © Atlantyca S.p.A. English translation © 2019 by Atlantyca S.p.A.

The publisher does not have any control over and does not assume any responsibility for author or third-party websites or their content.

GERONIMO STILTON and THEA STILTON names, characters, and related indicia are copyright, trademark, and exclusive license of Atlantyca S.p.A. All rights reserved. The moral right of the author has been asserted. Based on an original idea by Elisabetta Dami. geronimostilton.com

Published by Scholastic Inc., *Publishers since 1920*, 557 Broadway, New York, NY 10012. SCHOLASTIC and associated logos are trademarks and/or registered trademarks of Scholastic Inc.

Stilton is the name of a famous English cheese. It is a registered trademark of the Stilton Cheese Makers' Association. For more information, go to stiltoncheese.com.

No part of this publication may be reproduced, stored in a retrieval system, or transmitted in any form or by any means, electronic, mechanical, photocopying, recording, or otherwise, without written permission of the copyright holder. For information regarding permission, please contact: Atlantyca S.p.A., Via Leopardi 8, 20123 Milan, Italy; e-mail foreignrights@atlantyca.it, atlantyca.com.

This book is a work of fiction. Names, characters, places, and incidents are either the product of the author's imagination or are used fictitiously, and any resemblance to actual persons, living or dead, business establishments, events, or locales is entirely coincidental.

Library of Congress Cataloging-in-Publication Data available

ISBN 978-1-338-54701-6

Text by Thea Stilton
Original title *Il segreto delle fate delle stelle*
Cover by Iacopo Bruno, Caterina Giorgetti, Christian Aliprandi, and Giovanna Ferraris
Illustrations by Giuseppe Facciotto, Chiara Balleello, Barbara Pellizzari, Valeria Brambilla, and Alessandro Muscillo
Graphics by Daria Colombo

Special thanks to Tracey West
Translated by Julia Heim
Interior design by Kay Petronio

10 9 8 7 6 5 4 3 2 1   19 20 21 22 23

Printed in China   62

First edition, October 2019

THE THEA SISTERS

THEA   PAULINA   Colette

Violet   nicky   PAMELA

The Starlight Kingdom

Welcome to Starlight, the kingdom of the fairies of the stars! Fascinating creatures live in this world of shining stars. They are . . .

Astro: the ruler of Starlight, lives in Brightstar Castle. He governs over the stars and planets of the kingdom with justice, generosity, and courage.

Seven Fairy Cousins: are the cousins of Prince Astro. Thanks to their enchanted dance, the Starlight Kingdom lives in perfect harmony!

Cometta: is the master of harmony. Without her, the seven fairy cousins can't dance. And if they don't dance, the kingdom is in great danger.

Sixtar: protects all the deepest secrets of the starry night. She loves riddles and puzzles.

Glimmer Fairies: are very happy creatures and excellent cooks. They love hosting guests and delighting them with their starry treats!

Star Flower Elves: love plants and grow the precious glass flower, which reveals the purity of soul of whoever touches it.

Aphelia: is the fairy protector of time. She has been making hourglasses of all shapes and sizes since she was young.

Celestial Nymphs: are timid and delicate. They use herbs to prepare oils and teas with special powers.

Moon Gnome: does not like visitors. Whoever manages to reach his hiding place will be challenged to a magic checkers game.

Sirius: is a centaur who is very skilled with a bow and arrow. He lives on a faraway planet in the center of a labyrinth!

A VERY SPECIAL COURSE

It was a beautiful SUMMER day on Whale Island, the home of **MOUSEFORD ACADEMY**. The sun *shone* brightly in the blue sky, a warm wind blew, and the air smelled of the sea and **fLoweRS**.

It was the beginning of August, so most of all the students at the academy were taking a break from their studies and had gone on **VACATION**. The remaining students spent their free time relaxing in the classrooms, auditoriums, and gardens.

The Thea Sisters were all back at the academy that day. Nicky and Paulina *quickly* made their way toward the beach where Colette, Violet, and Pam were waiting for them. The five *friends* had plans to spend the day at the beach swimming, reading, and having a tasty **PICNIC**!

The two mouselets walked through the school's gardens. Colorful *flowers* were blooming, and insects and birds flitted among the plants.

"What a beautiful color!" Paulina exclaimed, pointing to a blue BUTTERFLY. "It reminds me of the sky back home in Peru."

The insect gently *flapped* its wings and flew away.

"Good-bye, butterfly!" Paulina rhymed. She bent down and breathed in the **scent** of the flowers, sighing. "I love summer!"

"Me, too," Nicky agreed. "And coming back to Mouseford for the seminar on constellations was a really **mousetastic** idea!"

"In a few days, we'll be able to see

Shooting stars are not stars, but meteors that burn when they move through the atmosphere. From Earth, you can see their light trails across the sky!

Shooting stars in the night sky," Paulina said.

"We should camp out in the garden," Nicky added. "I can't wait!"

Nicky and Paulina reached the beach. Seagulls flew overhead, calling out to one another. The mouselets spotted their friends by a red umbrella.

Colette and Violet were in their bathing suits, lying in the sun. Pam was busy building a sand castle with a big moat around it. She waved at Nicky and Paulina.

We'll see the stars!

"You made it!" she cried.

"**FINALLY!**" Colette exclaimed. "You really must try my new coconut-and-honey sunscreen. It's so **smooth**!

"Thanks, but I think I'll stay in the SHADE," Paulina said. She held up a book about **ASTRONOMY**. "I got this book from the library and I can't wait to start it!"

"I think I'll go for a swim," Nicky announced.

"I'll go with you!" Pamela cried. She jumped up, leaving her castle unfinished.

"Should we race to the buoy?" Nicky asked.

Pam grinned. "You're on!"

"Ready, set . . . go!" Nicky yelled. The mouselets raced to the ocean and jumped in.

"This is so relaxing," Violet said. "A nice day in the **sun** is just what we needed!"

"Definitely," Colette said, but Paulina didn't reply. Her **NOSE** was buried in her book.

"You're really **excited** for the seminar to start, aren't you, Paulina?" Violet remarked.

Paulina looked up and nodded, smiling.

"Seeing the **constellations** in the sky is so much more special than **LOOKING** at pictures in a book," she said.

Violet nodded. "That's true."

"Plus, we can each make a WISH on a shooting star!" Paulina added. "I think that's such a nice tradition."

"Shooting stars remind me of tiny fairies with sparkling outfits that light up the darkness of the night with their dance!" Colette commented with a **dreamy** look in her eyes.

"You're always so *romantic*, Coco!" Violet said, smiling. "But I'm looking forward to the shooting stars, too. I already have my LiST oF WiSHes!"

SOS, THEA SISTERS!

At the end of the day, the Thea Sisters returned to the academy. They closed their eyes on their couch, enjoying the **WARMTH** that they had brought with them from the beach.

"We had such a fabumouse day!" Violet commented.

"We did," Nicky said. "But now I need a long shower."

"I must get all this salt and sand out of my hair," Colette said. "I'll use the coconut shampoo, or maybe the avocado mask . . ."

"Mmmm, coconut and avocado," Pam said. "That sounds delicious!"

"Actually, that sounds gross," Nicky said, making a face.

"Maybe, but I'm hungry!" Pam replied, laughing.

The sound of a cell phone ringing interrupted them — but it was no ordinary cell phone. Surprised, all five friends looked toward the top drawer of the desk. It was always kept locked, because it contained the most **TOP SECRET** object that they owned: Will Mystery's cell phone.

Mouselets, it's Will!

Will had given it back to them at the end of their last mission so he could safely communicate secret information about their missions for the **SEVEN ROSES UNIT**.

"Do you think it's a new mission?" Pam asked, her eyes shining with excitement.

Paulina quickly opened the drawer with a tiny key and picked up the phone. Will's name **flashed** on the display.

"Hello, Will!" the Thea Sisters cried out.

"Hello, agents!" he replied. "It sounds like all five of you are there. That's **good**! I didn't think I would find you all at school."

"We all came back to Mouseford early from vacation to take a special class on CONSTELLATIONS."

"That is a very strange coincidence," Will said with a **MYsterIous** tone in his voice.

"Why? What's happening?" Colette asked.

"There is a problem with another one of the fantasy worlds," he said. "The *Starlight Kingdom*."

I need your help!

"Starlight?" Paulina repeated. "The **fantasy worlds** are all connected to places in the real world.

9

Is Starlight connected to the stars?"

"Yes, it is the home of the star fairies," he said. "But now their whole world is in danger."

"Oh no!" Violet exclaimed.

"What is the problem this time?" Pam asked.

"We have a few **CLUES**, but I will explain everything once you get to the base," Will responded. "This might be a secure line, but it is **risky** to give out details of SECRET missions over any phone."

"Of course, Will. When can you come get us?" Nicky asked.

"As soon as possible," Will replied. "There's no time to lose; Starlight is a particularly precious and fragile world, you'll see."

Paulina nodded. "Go ahead and send a HELICOPTER from the base. We will meet you in the park in an hour," she said.

"Are you sure no one will see you? It's still daylight," Will observed.

"The **SCHOOL** is practically deserted," Nicky reassured him.

"And in an hour, the few students who are here will all be getting ready for dinner," Pam added.

"Great! I'll see you here soon," Will said. "Thank you for being able to help on such short notice. You are an essential resource for the **SEVEN ROSES UNIT**."

"Um, how are we supposed to **pack** for a mission in under an hour?" Colette asked after they'd hung up.

Pam grabbed her by the paw. "We can do it. Come on!"

They *HURRIED* back to the rooms and quickly got ready. Colette showered and then started trying on clothes.

"What do you think?" she asked, twirling around in shorts and a sparkly, sequin-covered shirt. "Will this work for a visit to the Starlight Kingdom?"

"You look like you're going to a party, not a mission," Pam replied.

Nicky appeared at the door wearing khaki pants and a green cotton shirt. "Maybe something practical and simple might be better," she suggested.

What should I wear? Something practical!

Colette sighed. "I guess you're right."

They all packed *quickly*, and less than an hour later, they quietly made their way to the park.

They didn't have to wait long before the helicopter appeared in the clear sky above them. The **high-tech** vehicle made almost no noise as it landed.

The mouselets jumped on board.

"Fasten your seat belts," the pilot said. "I have **orders** to get you to the base with **MAXIMUM URGENCY**!"

As soon as the mouselets were ready, the helicopter **FLEW OFF** and away from Whale Island.

THE SEVEN ROSES UNIT

The headquarters of the Seven Roses Unit is hidden in the icy Arctic. Only the members of the unit know how to find the entrance.

THE ROSE PENDANT

Each researcher has a pendant that contains their personal information. It can be used as a key to open doors in the unit headquarters.

THE HALL OF THE SEVEN ROSES

In the heart of the unit is the Hall of the Seven Roses. It is a living map that shows every Fantasy World and reports on each one's condition. When a world is in danger, a crack appears in the map.

THE CRYSTAL ELEVATOR

A glass elevator is the gateway to the imaginary kingdoms. Only Will Mystery can operate the elevator using a special keyboard and a secret combination of musical notes. Then the power of music transports its occupants to a fantasy world!

A WORLD IN DANGER

The **super-silent** helicopter was also super fast, and they got to the **SECRET HEADQUARTERS** in no time.

Pam **GAZED** out the window as they approached the island in the frozen ocean. "Even though we've made this trip a bunch of times, it's always exciting!" she commented.

Then the helicopter picked up **SPEED**, and the Thea Sisters held their breath as it began a descent straight down onto the landing pad.

"This always makes me **DIZZY**!" Colette said.

"Steady, everyone!" the pilot called out, but he made a perfectly **smooth** landing. Through the windows, they could see Will Mystery impatiently pacing on the platform.

THE SEVEN ROSES UNIT

1. Landing platform
2. Elevator
3. Access to the surface
4. Hall of the Seven Roses
5. Supercomputer room
6. Relaxation area
7. Research laboratory
8. Clothing and supply room

"Will looks more worried than usual," Paulina remarked.

But Will's worried frown turned into a smile when the Thea Sisters emerged from the helicopter.

"**Welcome!**" he said, greeting them warmly. "How was the ride?"

"**PERFECT**, as always," Paulina replied.

Will thanked the pilot and led the mouselets to the exit.

"I want to apologize again for interrupting your **SUMMER**," he said. "I hope you will still be able to take part in your constellation class at Mouseford."

"It doesn't **START** for a few more days," Violet replied.

"And our priority is always the

well-being of the **fantasy worlds**," Paulina reassured him. "We know how important they are."

The others nodded in agreement.

"I'm glad to hear that," Will said.

Nicky spoke up. "You didn't say much on the phone about our new mission. What is the problem in the world of the Starlight Kingdom?"

"I'm going to explain everything soon," Will promised. "First I want to show you the situation in the **HALL OF THE SEVEN ROSES**."

He led the Thea Sisters down the stairs and into the Hall of the Seven Roses. This room held **magical maps** that showed all the fantasy worlds. When one was threatened by danger, a crack would open up on the map. A large **crack** could mean that the situation was very **serious**.

Will pointed to one of the maps. "As you can see, the crack in the Starlight Kingdom is already fairly large," he began. "The stars in this kingdom are powered by **LIGHT NESTS**, but something is causing the lights to go out. The stars are *losing* all their brightness and energy."

"Oh no!" Violet cried.

"How is that possible?" Paulina asked.

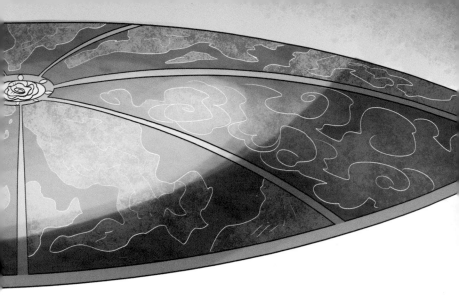

"The light nests produce a very special kind of **stardust** that powers the stars," Will explained. "But from what we can gather, this dust is running out."

Violet's eyes got wide. "So if there is no dust . . ."

"Then the stars may go **D A R K** forever," Will finished for her. "There is no time to lose."

"Then let's go!" Pam said **eagerly**.

"There is one thing we need to do before we leave," Will said. "Follow me, agents!"

A STELLAR MISSION

The Thea Sisters followed Will toward the clothing and supply room. Inside, there were outfits, gear, and equipment just right for a mission in every fantasy world.

"Our scientists have made some SPECIAL SUITS for this particular mission," Will explained. "You won't need space helmets, because Starlight exists in **magical** space. But these special suits will keep your body temperature stable and protect you from *space wind*."

He entered a code on the keypad on the wall. A door opened, revealing an orange-and-black space suit with matching boots.

"Fashionable *and* **PRACTICAL**," Colette remarked. "I love it!"

Will smiled. "I'm glad! Now please gear

up, agents, and I'll wait for you in the supercomputer room."

"I feel like a legit explorer!" Pam said, looking at her space suit.

When they met up with Will, the researcher was **BUSY** finishing up a report about the fantasy world of Starlight.

"I am almost finished compiling the **information** we will need for our journey," Will said. Then he **pressed** a button on the keyboard. **"Ready! Before we go, let's all read up about the star fairies.**

You will wear these suits!

"Cheese niblets! It sounds like an

WORLD OF STARLIGHT

POPULATION: A VARIETY OF CREATURES, INCLUDING FAIRIES OF THE STARS, ELVES, NYMPHS, GNOMES, AND STELLAR CENTAURS.

JOBS: THE FAIRIES OF THE STARS ARE THE WISE GUARDIANS OF THE ASTRAL LIGHT. THEY ARE FAMOUSE IN THE KINGDOM FOR THEIR ARTISTIC ABILITIES.

GOVERNMENT: PRINCE ASTRO IS KNOWN FOR HIS GREAT COURAGE, HIS KINDNESS OF HEART, AND HIS VALOR. HE RULES WITH THE HELP OF HIS SEVEN FAIRY COUSINS WHO ARE THE GUARDIANS OF COSMIC BALANCE: LUNARA, CELESTE, COSMIA, LYRE, PLEADIA, MAYA, AND ASTERIA.

LEGEND: IT IS SAID THAT PRINCE ASTRO'S FOREFATHERS BUILT BRIGHTSTAR CASTLE OUT OF STAR SAND, THE PUREST STARDUST THAT IS SHINIER THAN GOLD, SO THAT IT WOULD BE THE BRIGHTEST THING IN THE KINGDOM.

BRIGHTSTAR CASTLE:

THE PALACE MADE OF TALL, GLEAMING TOWERS THAT POINT TOWARD THE SKY LIKE THE POINTS ON A STAR. THE CASTLE IS BUILT ON A WHITE ROCK THAT CAN BE REACHED BY CLIMBING THE MOST DIFFICULT SILVER STAIRWAY, WITH STEPS THAT SHINE WITH PURE LIGHT. IT IS SURROUNDED BY THE STELLAR HEDGE, WHICH IS ADORNED WITH TINY, BRIGHT STARS.

HOW TO REACH BRIGHTSTAR:

TO REACH THE CASTLE YOU MUST FOLLOW THE STELLAR CONTRAIL AND CROSS THE BRIDGES OF LIGHT THAT UNITE THE PLANETS OF THE KINGDOM.

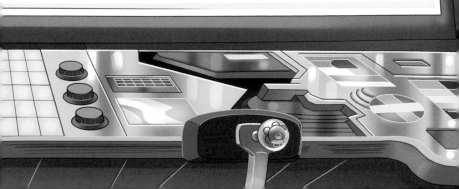

incredible place!" Pamela remarked, struck by what she had read on the computer screen.

"It is, just like all the other **fantasy worlds**," Will replied.

"And we will work hard to save it," Paulina said. "We will do everything we can."

Nicky nodded in agreement. "We can do it together!"

"Excellent! That is the **spirit** we need to face a mission as serious as this one," Will said. "Now it's time for me to suit up. Meet me at the CRYSTAL ELEVATOR in five minutes."

As soon as Will left the room, the friends exchanged **WORRIED** looks.

"I have a feeling that this might be our most **DIFFICULT MISSION** ever," Nicky said.

"We've been through some **TOUGH STUFF**

before, but we have always pulled through," Pam reminded her. "Will is counting on us. And so are all of the star fairies."

"You're right! We are the Thea Sisters!" Colette **shouted**. "We can do anything!"

The mouselets made their way to the Crystal Elevator.

As soon as they were all inside, Will played a special song on the keyboard. A very sweet melody began to *play*, surrounding the

CRYSTAL ELEVATOR. The music helped to calm the mouslets down a bit.

The elevator began to move, heading to . . .

Starlight, the kingdom of the Fairies of the stars!

A WORLD OF LIGHT

When the doors to the Crystal Elevator opened, a *RAY OF LIGHT* shone on them that was so intense Will and the Thea Sisters were forced to cover their eyes.

"I can't see anything!" Pam cried, shielding her face with her arm.

"We should be able to adjust to the light in a few minutes," Will assured them.

Trusting him, they **SLOWLY** opened their eyes. With each second, they were able to focus more and more until they could finally see the **astonishing** landscape of Starlight.

They stared at it **squeakless** for a few moments. Colorful planets hung in the dark sky overhead. Stars TWINKLED among them.

The elevator had landed on what looked

like a bridge of golden yellow light that connected the planets.

Will stepped out of the elevator onto the GOLDEN PATH. Paulina followed him.

"From here, this world seems endless," she remarked.

"It is very big, in fact. But we should be able to follow this star contrail to the Castle of Brightstar," Will said, pointing to a ribbon of **rainbow light** that sparkled down the bridge.

"What's a contrail?" Pam asked.

"On Earth, it's the trail left behind by a jet plane," Nicky replied.

Violet looked at the **computer** tablet she had brought with her. "According to the report, it's a bridge made of **stardust**."

Colette remembered something. "The report said that the castle is the **BRIGHTEST**

OBJECT in the sky, right?" she asked. "We should be able to spot it pretty easily."

"Let's look around," Nicky suggested.

"This world is so **amazing**," Paulina said, twirling around as she gazed at the planets. "When I think about these beautiful lights dying forever, it makes me so sad!"

Suddenly, her right foot slipped. She almost slid off the bridge, but Will **grabbed** her arm just in time.

"Got you!" he said. "This stardust is more *slippery* than we thought. I'll have to tell our equipment team to adjust the boots."

"No more twirling for me," Paulina said with a smile.

Then Colette called out from up ahead.

Are you okay?

Thanks!

"I think I've SPOTTED something!"

Everyone caught up to her.

"Can you see BRIGHTSTAR CASTLE from here?"
Will asked.

"I think so," Colette replied. She pointed to
a BRIGHT SPOT in the sky.

"Look, the bridge SPLITS OFF to the right,"
Nicky pointed out. "If we go that way, we
should be able to get closer."

Look!

They followed Nicky to that part of
the bridge. It became narrower
and steeper as they walked,
and they landed on a
glowing blue star. Up
ahead, another colorful contrail led
to a bright silver object in the sky.

"That must be Brightstar," Will
said. "Nice work, Nicky!"

He looked at the rainbow ribbon

leading them to the silver light in the sky.

"We need to be even more CAREFUL as we move forward," he said. "We could run into some TROUBLE on the way to Brightstar."

"What kind of trouble?" Pam asked.

Before Will could answer, a sudden **gust of air** struck Pam and almost knocked her over. The cape on her space suit billowed up around her, helping her to keep her balance.

"Holey cheese, it's WINDY out here!" Pam exclaimed.

"That was a **STELLAR CURRENT**," Will explained. "We know that they are pretty common in Starlight, which is why your space suits are equipped to help you keep your balance, even in extreme circumstances."

"Well, I'm sure glad it worked," Pam declared, laughing.

"So these capes aren't just there to make

the suits look cute," Colette remarked.

"We need to be **extra careful** as we move on," Paulina said.

"Follow me," Will instructed. He stepped on the ledge, and the **expedition** continued.

The Thea Sisters carefully made their way

It's incredible!

What a sight!

along the bridge, but they couldn't help looking around in admiration. They became more and more certain that . . .

they would do whatever it took to save that unique world!

This way!

THE GUARDIAN FAIRY OF THE NIGHT

Will and the Thea Sisters kept walking. The bridge curved upward, and when they got to the top, the light of **BRIGHTSTAR CASTLE** still seemed so far away.

"This starlight pathway keeps twisting and turning," Nicky remarked. "It's going to take **FOREVER** to reach the castle!"

"It appears that way," Will said. "It's odd that the computer didn't **WARN** us about this."

Paulina looked down the slope. "Wait, what's that?" she asked. "There's another star between here and the castle."

At the bottom of the slope was a star that gave off a cold, **metallic** light. Violet shivered.

"Just looking at that planet gives me the **chills**," she said.

"Me, too," Colette said. "I don't know why but something doesn't feel right."

"Yeah, it's **CREEPY**," Pam said. "Is there any way to avoid it?"

"I'm afraid there's no other way to the castle, unfortunately," Will declared. "But let's keep our eyes OPEN."

They all followed Will down the slope. As soon as they stepped onto the **strange** star, a gust of freezing air struck them.

Violet shivered again. "Okay, now I have the *other* kind of chills!"

"*IT'S SO COLD!*" Colette complained, hugging her shoulders. "Let's *hurry* and get to the next bridge of starlight!"

"I don't mind the cold so much," Paulina said.

Keep moving!

Brrr · · ·

"It reminds me of the snowy mountains back home. But I agree with Pam — there is definitely something **spooky** about this star!"

They walked through a frozen, deserted wasteland, following the path of **rainbow light** that crossed over the star. Silver-gray rocks covered the star's surface, and a beautiful metallic, shimmering dust swirled all around them.

"Look down there!" Nicky cried out suddenly, pointing to something in the distance. "It's a weird-looking building."

"It's shaped like a **globe**," Colette said. "And the starlight path goes right through it!"

"Can't we go **around** it?" Violet asked.

Will shook his head. "The contrail is magical. It appeared when we arrived here, but if we **stray** from the path, it will disappear.

We'd never find it again."

"I guess we have to go, then," Paulina concluded.

They walked right toward the **strange** building, following the contrail. It didn't take long to reach it, but Will stopped suddenly when they were just a few steps from it.

"That's strange," he said. "There doesn't appear to be a door."

They walked all the way around it, looking for a way in.

"It's a smooth surface with no opening," Paulina observed. "How is that possible?"

Nicky knocked on the building with her paw. "It feels like SOLID METAL, as a matter of fact," she said.

"How are we supposed to follow the contrail through the building?" Colette asked, confused. "It makes no sense."

"Now what do we do?" Violet wondered.

Will put his paw on his chin. "This is definitely a TRICKY situation," he said. "When I did my report, I . . ."

A loud laugh interrupted him.

A slice of the globe-shaped wall in front of them became transparent, and the mysterious figure of a woman appeared. She wore a blue crown of stars, and more stars glittered on her blue gown.

"Pay no attention to me," she said. "Please CONTINUE as you were. I am having a ton of fun listening to your silly logic as you try to figure out my sphere."

"This is your sphere? Who are you?" Colette asked.

"My name is SIXTAR, and I am the fairy guardian of the starry night," she answered. "Who are you? Where do you come from, and why are you here on **MY STAR**?"

"We are following the stellar contrail to reach the palace of Brightstar," Will explained.

"Do you intruders really think you can just march into the castle?" she asked.

"We aren't intruders! We are here to save

It is the fate of your world!

Starlight!" Pam answered, offended.

"I do not remember INVITING you onto my star," Sixtar said. "That makes you intruders!"

"But we're trying to help you!" Pam said.

Colette stepped toward her. "Don't you even care about the fate of your world? You are heartless!" she said angrily.

The two of them stood **Face-to-Face** on either side of the transparent wall and exchanged challenging looks.

"I must confess you are very brave, young one, to face a fairy of the night like myself," Sixtar said. "That's why I will let you cross my star."

She waved her arm, and the transparent wall slid open.

"Hooray!" Pam cheered. "We can go!"

"Not so fast," Sixtar said coldly. "To

continue along your path you must pass a **test**."

"I should have known," Pam muttered. "Fairies love tests and riddles!"

"What kind of **test**?" Will asked Sixtar.

Sixtar smiled. "You will soon find out."

"And if we pass the test, do you PROMISE to let us pass through your sphere?" Paulina asked.

Sixtar's eyes narrowed. "How dare you doubt my word!"

Will and the Thea Sisters were not sure they could trust Sixtar, but they had no choice. So, after exchanging nods of agreement, they prepared for . . .

the test of the
fairy guardian
of the night.

THE RIDDLE OF THE SILVER VASES

As soon as they crossed through the entrance of that mysterious building, the Thea Sisters and Will found themselves inside a vault with images of glowing stars and **PLANETS** all around them. The guardian fairy waited with her arms folded for the group to reach the center of the dome.

"Are you ready to face your test?" she asked.

"We are ready," Colette confirmed. "And we're in a bit of a hurry."

"How sweet. Do you really think that you'll get through this quickly?" Sixtar asked sharply. Then she WAVED her hands once more in the air, pronounced some strange words, and SNAPPED her fingers.

In a flash, a group of **silver** objects appeared in front of Will and the Thea Sisters.

Two silver jars sat on the floor, next to a large silver scale with two plates. Four **golden stars** were next to the scale.

"This is your first test," she began. "These four stars weigh four pounds. I will put them on one plate of the scale. You must balance the scale by putting exactly four pounds of sand on the scale. One of these jars contains five pounds of sand. The other contains three pounds. Figuring out how to measure exactly four pounds of sand is your test!"

Will and the Thea Sisters exchanged confused looks. They hadn't expected such a difficult **TEST**.

"I think this problem calls for a math whiz," Colette said. "That would be you, Paulina."

Paulina nodded. "There is a SOLUTION for every problem. We just have to try."

"That is not all," Sixtar continued. "The vase with the exact amount of sand must be placed on the scale. You can't add or take sand away until the plates are balanced. Furthermore —"

"Galloping gears! There's more?" Pam asked.

"—You must pass the test before one hourglass runs out," Sixtar added with a mocking grin.

"And if we don't?" Will asked.

"If you don't, you can't continue and you will remain prisoners in this dome . . . **forever**!" she threatened. Then she disappeared with a piercing laugh.

"Okay, we all need to work together on this," Will said. "But, Paulina, we're counting on you to lead the way. We need to answer this RIDDLE as quickly as we can!"

Paulina nodded. "I think we can do it." She took out her notebook.

"Let's REVIEW the rules," Will began. "We have two vases. One has three pounds of sand, and the other has five pounds. We need to put four pounds of sand in one vase so it can **BALANCE** with the stars on the scale."

"We could put the vase with five pounds on the scale, and then take out the extra sand until it balances," Pam suggested.

"Sixtar was clear: We can't do ANYTHING while the vase is on the scale," Will reminded her.

"There must be another way," Paulina said, tapping her pencil on her notebook.

Colette spoke up. "Let's think about this one step at a time," she said. "We know that we're going to have to use the **bigger vase** on the scale. The smaller vase will never fit four pounds of sand."

"Okay, that's a start," Violet said. "We could empty the big vase and fill it with the sand from the little one. Then we would know for sure that there are three pounds of sand in the big one."

"Right," Colette said. "But then we'd need to add exactly **one more pound**. And we have no way to measure that exactly."

"But I think we're onto something," Nicky said hopefully. "Five pounds minus one pound is four pounds. Three plus one is four. It's all in the math. The key is in figuring out that **one pound**!"

Paulina had been busy writing in her

notebook. "I think I've got it," she said. "First, we empty the **five-pound** jar and pour the contents of the **three-pound** jar in it, like Colette said."

"Got it so far," Pam said.

"Then, we fill up the **three-pound** jar with the sand we just dumped out of the other jar," Paulina continued. "That leaves us with three pounds of sand in each jar."

"Okay, but we still need to figure out how to *measure* one pound," Colette said.

Paulina smiled. "Easy! We will pour the contents of the **three-pound** jar into the **five-pound** jar until it's full. We will be pouring two pounds of sand into the five-pound jar. So

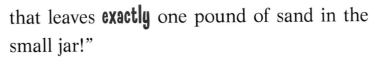

that leaves **exactly** one pound of sand in the small jar!"

"I get it!" Violet exclaimed. "Then we dump out the five-pound jar. We POUR the one pound of sand into it. Then we fill up the three-pound jar again and add it to the five-pound jar. Three plus one is four!"

"Exactly!" Paulina cried.

"HOORAY!" everyone cheered.

Will pointed to the silver hourglass. "Let's hurry and get it done. Time is running out!"

They all worked together, filling and emptying the vases until they had exactly four pounds of sand in the big vase. Then Paulina and Colette carefully placed it on the empty plate on the scale.

The instant that the last grain of sand fell from the top of the hourglass, the two plates reached the perfect **balance**.

Will and the Thea Sisters breathed a huge sigh of relief: They had done it!

A moment later, Sixtar appeared before them in a whirlwind of silver dust. Seeing the puzzle solved, her icy eyes widened. "You did it!" she exclaimed.

"Every problem has a solution," Paulina repeated. "Even the hardest ones."

"Very few have solved it before you," Sixtar answered.

"Now you have to keep your **PROMISE**," Colette reminded her. "Let us pass through your dome, and follow the starlight path."

The FAIRY hesitated, still in disbelief of what had happened.

"I always keep my promises," she said coldly. Then she raised her arms in the air and made a lightning-fast gesture.

"You may pass!"

After she uttered the words, a new gap OPENED in the

other side of the wall. Will and the Thea Sisters saw the glittering starlight contrail on the other side.

Will stepped out of the dome. "Follow me, agents!"

The Thea Sisters quickly said good-bye to the fairy guardian and followed Will out of the dome. The contrail led them to a new golden bridge that stretched across the *BLUE SKY*.

"I can't wait to get out of here," Pam remarked.

"I think we're getting closer," Will said. "I can see the Light of Brightstar in the distance."

They all walked on . . .

toward the heart of the Starlight Kingdom!

THE DELIGHTFUL GLIMMER FAIRIES

"It feels good to be back on the move," Nicky said as they made their way along the bridge of light.

"I was **afraid** we wouldn't pass Sixtar's test," Violet admitted.

"I knew we could count on Paulina!" Colette said, and Paulina smiled at her friend.

"I couldn't have done it without everyone's help," Paulina said.

"We do make a great team," Will said. "That's why I chose the five of you to come to Starlight. Every one of you has a different strength."

He smiled at Paulina. "Your math skills were definitely **the star** of this part of the mission."

"Thanks, Will," she replied.

"I have a feeling we'll all be put to the test," Pam remarked. "I've never met a fairy who didn't like to test strangers!"

Will nodded. "There will be more challenges, I'm sure," he agreed. "Let's get to **BRIGHTSTAR** and see what awaits us there."

They continued on the bridge. It twisted and **turned** across the starry sky. They climbed up another slope, and as they headed down, they saw another star ahead of them. It glimmered with a warm, happy glow.

Great job!

Thanks!

"How pretty!" Violet exclaimed. "This star looks a lot more CHEERFUL than Sixtar's star."

Nicky walked up beside her. The star **pulsed** with warm colors of pink, **blue**, and **purple**. "You can say that again," she said. "I'm looking forward to seeing what's on this star."

"I have a feeling that whoever lives on this star is very *happy*," Paulina remarked.

"I hope so," Pam said. "Happy fairies usually don't give impossible tests to strangers! And they usually have good food."

She patted her stomach, which **rumbled** with hunger. Everyone laughed.

"I suppose we'll find out soon enough," Colette said.

"That's my Pam. Only you could think about food in the middle of a **MAGICAL** space land," Nicky said.

"We've been walking on this bridge for a long time," Pam said. "Of course I'm hungry."

She paused. "Isn't there a saying that the moon is made of **green cheese**?" she asked. "I could go for some cheese right now.

I don't care what **color** it is!"

They reached the end of the bridge and stepped onto the pretty star. They walked across the green, hilly land. The green trees that dotted the landscape all seemed to sparkle. Bubbling brooks flowed through the land, and their blue water seemed to sparkle, too.

"This is cool!" Nicky said. "The stars we learn about at Mouseford are made of gas. But here they are their own little MAGICAL worlds!"

They climbed a hill and saw a village in the valley below them. The unusual-looking buildings were yellow, pink, blue, and purple, and were topped with tall towers.

Nicky pointed. "Look, there are flying creatures over there, and they're sparkling!" she said.

"This looks like a village, and those must be fairies," Will said.

"To follow the starlight trail, we need to cross the valley," Pam pointed out.

"I think it looks safe," Will said. "Let's go."

As they made their way into the village, they heard the sound of flapping wings behind them. Then they heard a cheerful voice.

"Good morning, and welcome!" chirped a happy-looking fairy as she flew in front of them.

The fairy was **small**, about half the size of any of the Thea Sisters. She wore a pretty blue hat with yellow stars on it, and a **big smile** lit up her face.

Welcome, travelers!

"Good morning, kind fairy," Will greeted her. "We are sorry to disturb you, but we are headed to BRIGHTSTAR CASTLE. We are following the stellar contrail and need to cross through your village to continue on our way."

"You are **WELCOME**," she replied in a pleasant voice. "It's always a great pleasure for us to receive guests. Visitors are so rare these days."

"We know the situation in your *kingdom*," Will said. "We are here to try to help you."

The small fairy **FROWNED**, but it quickly turned into a *smile* again.

"You must visit our village this evening while you are here," she said. "We make the most delicious starry cuisine."

"I knew it! **HOORAY!**" Pam cheered.

"We would love to stay," Will said.

"Then follow me," the fairy said.

"Just one question," Pam said. "Do you have any green cheese?"

A STARRY MENU

The fairy giggled at Pam's question. "I am not sure what that is, but I think you will find we have some *delectable* treats to share."

She led them farther into the village.

"Where are we, exactly?" Colette asked.

"In Glimmer Village!" the fairy replied. "I am **BLUESTAR**, a glimmer fairy."

She called out to another fairy who was close by. "**VIOLETSTAR**, come, we have guests!"

The second fairy also had a welcoming

Pleased to meet you!

smile. "It's good to meet you! What a nice surprise. I will go and tell the other fairies at once!" She **flew** off toward the colorful houses of the village and returned with a dozen other fairies.

"This is a very happy place," Paulina observed.

"Oh, yes, happiness is very important to us!" Bluestar said. "Now, let us take you to the feast!"

The fairies grabbed the *paws* of the visitors and lifted them off the ground. Then they soared through the village.

"What a sight!" Paulina exclaimed.

"They are taking us to the biggest building," Violet figured out.

"This is where GOLDSTAR lives," Bluestar said. "She will handle the Starry Buffet for the big dinner tonight."

They landed at the entrance to a round pink building.

A fairy wearing golden yellow was consulting a giant cookbook. She smiled when she saw them.

"**Welcome!**" she said.

"Goldstar, these are our GUESTS," Bluestar announced.

"We are happy to have you taste our starry cooking," the fairy responded. Then she called out, "Orangestar, Greenstar, **quick**!"

Two more fairies appeared.

"Please add six extra places at the table, and bring out the DESSERT cart," Goldstar instructed.

"Yes, Goldstar," the two fairies replied, and they quickly flew off.

Goldstar nodded to **BLUESTAR**. "Please take them to the dining room."

Bluestar led the guests through a big door into the **BANQUET** hall.

Happy to meet you!

"Galloping gears!" Pam exclaimed

as soon as she stepped into the room. "Is this real?"

Inside the room was an ENORMOUSE table set for a fancy dinner. It was topped with bowls and trays OVERFLOWING with food that looked delicious!

"We will never be able to taste it all!" Colette remarked, looking at all the dishes.

"I promise to do my best," Pam replied, WINKING at her friends. "I wouldn't want to INSULT the fairies!"

Violet approached the table. "Look," she said. "Every plate has a card next to it with the name of the food written on it."

"Each looks TASTIER than the next," Paulina remarked.

"Make yourselves comfortable," Bluestar said, pointing to six seats. "The banquet of the stars will begin shortly!"

> ✦ **A**STRAL PASTRY WITH
> STARFRUIT SAUCE ✦

Right after they sat down, **GOLDSTAR** and the other fairies joined them.

"What a beautiful party," Violet remarked. "Isn't that right, Pam?"

But Pam, who was next to her, had her mouth full of food.

> ✦ **G**ALAXY SALAD
> SPRINKLED WITH
> CURRIED COMET DUST ✦

Pam just nodded her head. "Mmm hmmfff!" she replied, and her **friends** burst out laughing.

They tried one tasty dish after another. Paulina had to put her fork down. "I can't eat another bite," she whispered to Nicky.

"Thank you, Goldstar. Everything was *delicious*," Will told the cook.

> ✦ **S**TAR-SHAPED ROLLS
> WITH CELESTIAL ROSE
> CREAM AND LARGE
> FLAKES OF CHOCOLATE ✦

Goldstar grinned. "I am so pleased."

"Hooray!" CHEERED the fairy helpers.

They all clapped their hands, and hundreds of colorful SPARKS flew up in the air.

A moment later, loud CRACKLING sounds could be heard from outside. Colorful lights began to SHINE on the other side of the large windows of the banquet hall.

Nicky clapped her paws together. "A FIREWORKS show! Awesome."

Bluestar motioned to the guests. "Let's go OUTSIDE and enjoy the show," she said, and they followed her out of the banquet hall to a large terrace.

The fireworks lit up the sky with magical colors, lights, and music.

After the show, the glimmer fairies led their guests to cozy cabins, where they all slept on soft, comfy beds. When they awoke the next morning, they got MOVING right away.

They said good-bye to Goldstar, and **BLUESTAR** accompanied them as they followed the STARLightt ribbon to the next bridge.

But when they got to the bridge, it was split in two.

"Which way should we go?" Pam asked.

Colette squinted into the distance. "I think I see **BRIGHTSTAR** this way," she said, **pointing** to the bridge on the right.

"Thank you so much for all your help, Bluestar," Paulina said.

"And for all the *good food*," Pam added.

You are welcome," Bluestar replied. "Good luck with your **journey**. I hope you can save the Starlight Kingdom!"

"We will do our best," Paulina promised, and then they all stepped onto the *BRIDGE OF LIGHT*.

THE NYMPH'S QUESTION

Pam chattered on and on about the food in Glimmer Village.

Violet laughed. "Well, maybe there'll be more food for you when we get to Brightstar," she said.

Colette sighed. "I'm starting to wonder if we will ever get to Brightstar. We've been walking for hours."

"This BRIDGE OF LIGHT seems to be much longer than the others," Will agreed.

"It kind of feels like we're in the middle of nowhere," Nicky added. "Like the Australian Outback, but in space."

They gazed around. Except for the light of BRIGHTSTAR in the distance, there were no colorful planets or stars on this part of the bridge.

They walked along in silence after that. The bridge **twisted** to the right, and when they followed the CURVE, they could see a strange structure on the horizon.

"Is that a road?" Violet asked. "I think I saw a row of **lampposts**."

They soon reached the end of the bridge, which put them on the surface of a very shiny star.

"Look!" Colette cried, pointing. "There are stars inside those lamps!"

It was true. Streetlights lined the road. On top of each tall golden pole was a glass globe, and inside each globe was a burning star!

"Even the field seems to shimmer with golden sparkles," Paulina noted.

"So does the building at the end of this road," Colette observed.

"What do you think we'll find inside?" Pam wondered.

Overcome by a strong sense of CUriOSiTy, they hurried down the road. When they got closer, they realized that the building looked like a large greenhouse made of **glass** and **METAL**. The entrance to the greenhouse was a double-paned glass door framed with SILVER.

Paulina tried to open the doors. "They're locked!" she announced.

"Of course they are," Nicky remarked. "Nothing **works** the way it's supposed to in a fairy world."

"So, what do we do?" Violet said, asking the **QUESTION** that was on everyone's mind.

"It's easy, dear guests. You just need to answer a simple question," a little voice said from above them.

Will jumped. "Who said that?"

"I did, obviously," the little voice answered.

Everyone in the group looked up, **down**, and **around**, but they didn't see anyone.

"Up here! I'm here, on the lamppost to your right!" the voice said.

That's when they finally spotted her: a tiny fairy with long blonde hair. She was no bigger than a flower.

"A mini fairy!" Violet exclaimed.

"I am a nymph of the stars, to be precise," the small creature replied. "My name is Luminasia. Who are you?"

"It's nice to meet you," Violet said. "We are traveling to Brightstar."

"I am the guardian of the greenhouse of the **glass flowers**," Luminasia said.

"What are **glass flowers**?" Colette wanted to know.

The nymph looked surprised. "You really don't know them? They are the most beautiful flowers in the kingdom. They reflect the LIGHT OF THE STARS and the pure spirit of whoever is holding them. They are extremely *rare, fragile, and precious*."

"They must be very special. Can we see them?" Violet asked.

"Possibly," the nymph replied. "They are EXTREMELY DELICATE. Only the elves know the secret to growing them."

rare, fragile, and precious

"Elves?" Pam asked.

"The **star flower elves** are the most expert and capable gardeners of the kingdom," the nymph explained.

"How *interesting*!" Paulina said. "Can we meet them?"

Luminasia looked at them for a moment. "I suppose so. But to enter the greenhouse, you must answer my **RIDDLES** correctly," she said.

"More riddles," Nicky whispered to Pam.

"We agree to your terms," Will told the nymph.

Luminasia smiled. "You must guess the word that is made up of the answers to these two riddles:

"1. What gets everything wet when it gets sad and lights up our lives when it's feeling glad?"

"2. If you have two dots, well, that's just fine, but to put them together you need a . . . ?"

The Thea Sisters huddled together.

"Let's start with the **FIRST RIDDLE**," Pam said. "What gets everything wet when it's **SAD** and lights up when it's feeling glad?"

"Rain makes everything wet," Violet said.

"And when it's done raining, the SUN comes out," Colette added.

Violet grinned. "So could the answer be . . . the sky?"

"That's got to be it!" Nicky cried. "Now we just need to solve the **SECOND RIDDLE**. If you have two dots, well that's just fine, but to put them together, you need a . . . what?"

"Well, the easiest way to CONNECT two dots with a pencil is to draw a line," Paulina said.

"To put them together, you need a line," Nicky said. "That's it!"

"Well done, Paulina " Colette said.

"So, the first word is *sky*," Violet said.

"And the second is *line*," Paulina finished.

"Skyline!" the five friends all called out at once.

The tiny fairy's face burst into a grin.

She flew over to the greenhouse door, took a small **crystal key** from her pocket, and then inserted it into a TINY lock and opened the doors.

"Please come in," Luminasia said.

They stepped inside and GASPED. A golden pathway led through the greenhouse. All around them bloomed colorful, SHIMMERING flowers.

"It's so beautiful!" Violet exclaimed.

THE VERY RARE GLASS FLOWER

Colette took a deep breath inside the greenhouse. "Can you all **smell** that? It is nicer than any perfume I've ever owned."

"It almost smells **BETTER** than food — almost," Pam said.

"What you are smelling is the scent of the **glass flower**," a melodious voice answered them.

They turned to their right to see an **elf** standing there. He wasn't tiny, like the **NYMPH**, but the same size as them. He had long yellow hair and wore green clothing with a matching apron.

Beside him was a shelf of pots with newly sprouted plants growing in them. The plants all had colorful buds.

"Good morning," Will said. "Are you one of the **STAR FLOWER ELVES** that Luminasia told us about?"

"That's right," the elf replied. "My name is **LEROY**. Who are you? And why are you here?"

Will introduced them all and explained their mission. "We need to reach **BRIGHTSTAR CASTLE** as soon as possible so that we can speak to *Prince Astro*," Will concluded.

The elf listened to the whole tale with a serious expression.

"I understand," he said. "We are all very *worried* about what is happening in our **kingdom**. The stars of Starlight are a little less bright every day, and the survival of our people, as well as that of our beloved plants, depends on their light."

"What do you mean?" Paulina asked.

"All the species that you see here, including the precious **glass flower**, feed off the light of the stars," Leroy explained. "Then they reflect that light throughout the kingdom."

"So without the **STARLIGHT**, these plants would disappear?" Violet asked.

The elf nodded sadly.

"**Don't worry**, Leroy. We are here to help you," Colette said, trying to reassure him.

Leroy nodded. "My companions and I would be eternally **grateful**."

"If it's not too much trouble, can we please see a **glass flower** up close before we go on our way?" Violet asked.

"Of course," the elf responded. He asked the mice to follow him. He led them to a display case in the middle of the **greenhouse**. Growing inside pots were shining flowers with large petals. They looked like they were made entirely of glass.

"**Cheese niblets!** I've never seen anything like this!" Pam exclaimed.

This is a very a rare species with **ANCIENT ORIGINS**," Leroy explained. "Cultivating these flowers takes a lot of care — but most of all, STARLIGHT is essential for them to grow."

"Luminasia told us that these flowers can reflect the pure spirit of whoever holds them," Colette remembered.

"It's true — you can try it yourself," the elf said as he opened the case. "Reach out and touch one of the petals.

Colette approached the plant and did what Leroy had instructed. As soon as her paw touched the flower, the transparent petals turned a beautiful shade of PINK. Everyone stared in amazement.

"The flower has recognized your **romantic** spirit and your favorite color!" Violet exclaimed.

"Can I try, too?" Nicky asked. Leroy nodded, and she *touched* a petal as well.

The flower immediately turned a delicate shade of **green**, the color of nature that Nicky loved so much.

Then it was Pam's turn, and the flower turned **RED**, a color full of *positivity* and **energy**, just like her!

For Violet, the petals turned a very delicate **lilac**, almost the color of her name.

When it was finally Paulina's turn, the glass flower turned an intense orange color, which reminded her of a beautiful sunset.

"Will, now it's your turn,"

Paulina concluded, turning to the head of the **SEVEN ROSES UNIT** with a smile.

Will stared at the flowers for a moment. Then he reached out and touched one of them. Immediately the petals turned a bright light blue that shone like the summer sky.

"That color represents the spirit of a dreamer and someone who strives to do good," Leroy announced. "Now I know why you and your team were called to save our world. You mice are a great team."

"**Hooray!**" the Thea Sisters all cried out.

Just then another **elf** dressed in green walked up to them.

The elf wore a hat that was taller than Leroy's, and he had a very long **BEARD**.

"This is Silmon, the oldest and wisest elf in the village," Leroy said, introducing him. Then he motioned to Will and the Thea Sisters. "Silmon, these are the mice who have come to HELP Starlight. The glass flower has shown them to be pure of spirit."

"I am happy to hear that, and pleased to welcome you to our village," Silmon said. "The situation on Starlight, unfortunately, is quite serious; we need all the help we can get."

"It is an honor for us to be here," Will replied. "We will try our best to help you solve

Welcome!

the **PROBLEM** that threatens Starlight — you have our word. But to do so, we need to reach **BRIGHTSTAR CASTLE**."

"You're almost there," Silmon said. "There is just one more **obstacle** that awaits you."

"What is it?" Colette asked.

"It is a **giant** who answers to the name of Sphericon," Silmon answered. "He is the guardian of the Silver Gate, the entry to the SILVER STAIRWAY."

"We read about the stairway back at unit headquarters!" Paulina remembered. "But the computer didn't say anything about a giant. Is he a **nice** giant?" she asked hopefully.

"He can be, when he is in a GOOD MOOD," the elf answered. "But most of the time he is not. In case he makes it difficult for you, I will give you an object that will serve as your gate **pass**."

"So if we give him the gift, he'll open gate?" Pam asked.

"Yes, but it isn't just any old gift. It is a **THOUSAND-LIGHT GEM**. It is quite valuable, and only a few exist. Here it is."

He held out his hand and gave Colette a small glass dome with a colorful CRYSTAL FLOWER inside.

"Thank you," Will said. "This will be a big help."

"You're welcome. Now go!" Silmon said, pointing to the exit. The door opened, and they could see the star contrail sparkling on the other side.

SPHERICON THE GIANT

They followed the contrail to the next bridge of light. Colette held the **THOUSAND-LIGHT GEM** like it was a precious treasure. Not only was it their pass to get onto the Silver Stairway, but it was also a flower of **rare beauty**.

"It is really the **brightest** gem I've ever seen!" Paulina observed, gazing at the crystal flower.

"It changes when the light touches it," Colette told her. "There must be a thousand shades of color in this crystal!"

The others gathered around Colette to get a better look. They were all struck by the **beauty** of the marvelous gem.

"If this doesn't put that giant in a **GOOD**

MOOD, I don't know what will!" Pam remarked.

They walked until they came to a blue fog. After they passed through it, a surprising LANDSCAPE opened up before their eyes. For the first time, they could see **BRIGHTSTAR CASTLE** shining on the horizon in all its **SPLENDOR**.

Paulina let out a cry.

"I can see the Silver Gate down there!"

"That's where the giant is waiting for us," Nicky said. "And you can see the SILVER STAIRWAY through the gate."

"We're almost there!" Pam cheered.

The bridge of light came to a **STOP** right in front of the two large silver doors.

"What now?" Pam asked.

"Should we try to **knock**?" Nicky proposed.

Paulina pointed to a silver chain hanging from the gate. "This might be a BELL," she said. "Should we try pulling it?"

"Give it a try," Will advised.

Paulina grabbed the end of the chain and pulled it, cautiously. A loud chime rang out. Then came the sound of **heavy** footsteps.

"Who disturbs my peace?" a voice thundered from the other side of the gate. The door creaked open, pulled by a giant hand.

The giant hand belonged to an ENORMOUSE

creature who was three times as tall as the mice. He wore a silver helmet on his head, and a large, **furry** beard grew from his face.

Will bravely stepped forward. "Good day, Sphericon," he said in his friendliest voice.

The giant's eyes narrowed with SUSPICION. "Who are you and how do you know my name?" he asked.

Colette spoke up. "Why, Sphericon, don't you know how famouse you are? Everyone in Starlight knows of the **great guardian** of the Silver Gate. Your name is known throughout the kingdom!"

"She's flattering him. Nice!" Pam whispered to Nicky.

Sphericon reflected for a few seconds, and then the **SHARP** expression on his big bearded face sweetened.

"I suppose you are right," he said, in a less

GROUCHY tone. "But I would still like to know what you are doing here."

"We are making our way to **BRIGHTSTAR CASTLE**," Paulina answered.

"Prince Astro is waiting for us," Pam added.

The giant **frowned** and shook his big, shaggy head.

"I'm sorry, but you can't pass through here," he responded.

"But there is no other path!" Violet pleaded.

"I know, but that makes no difference. You can't pass through here!" he

repeated, more firmly this time.

Colette reached out and held up the **glass** dome that the elves had given her with the **CRYSTAL** flower inside.

"We have a gift for you, great Sphericon," she said.

The giant took the *fragile* dome from her paw and stared at its contents for a moment, turning it in his hands, confused.

Then he recognized the gem and his eyes widened.

A thousand-light gem!

"But this is a **THOUSAND-LiGHT GEM**," he said. "I've never seen one so close up before."

"The star flower elves gave it to us," Will Mystery explained. "As a pass to be able to get to the castle."

"The gem shines with a thousand sparkles," Sphericon **OBSERVED** in admiration. "This means that it has been feeding off the **energy** of your pure hearts."

"Accept it as a gift and let us pass, please, Sphericon," Colette said.

"We're on a mission to **save** the kingdom of Brightstar," Pam added.

Sphericon looked down at the gem. "Now I have **proof** that you are telling the truth, and that you come in friendship. And so, I will let you pass."

"Thank you so much," Colette said.

He motioned for them to pass, and they began the long **climb** up the steep Silver Stairway that led to **BRIGHTSTAR CASTLE**!

WELCOME TO BRIGHTSTAR

The stairway went up and up and up, until they finally reached the tall, beautiful castle. It was made of gleaming blue stone, and a soft yellow light glowed from within.

"What a sight!" Violet cried as they approached.

The castle entrance was a BIG BLUE DOOR decorated with star-shaped carvings. Will lifted his paw to knock, but before he could touch it, the door opened on its own. Inside stood two elegant, smiling fairies ready to greet them.

"Welcome, dear guests," they said in unison, bowing.

"Thank you, **kind fairies**," Colette replied. "We are here to see Prince Astro."

The two fairies nodded. "We would be happy to take you to him. Follow us, please."

They led the visitors through a vast hallway, to a door that opened into the throne room.

"Prince Astro is waiting for you," the two fairies said, speaking in unison once more. "You can enter, please."

"Thank you," Will responded, and they stepped inside the throne room. There, beneath a velvet, STAR-STUDDED canopy, a young, worried-looking prince sat on a crystal throne.

As soon as he saw the mice, he rose to his feet and went to meet them with a sad smile.

"WELCOME, FRIENDS!" he said in a kind voice. "I am Prince Astro."

Will bowed his head. "It is great honor to meet you, Your Majesty. I am Will Mystery, and these are my colleagues."

"I'm sorry Sphericon stopped you, but he had noble intentions," Prince Astro explained. "His job is to protect this palace and make sure that only PURE-HEARTED visitors like you approach!"

"He was actually a pretty NICE GIANT," Pam assured him.

"I thank you for being here," the prince continued. "As you know, the situation in Starlight is getting **worse**, and nothing I can do will fix it."

"Don't be sad, Prince. That is why we are here to help you," Paulina said. "We know you can't do this alone."

"We know that the *LIGHT* of the stars in your world is going out, but we don't **UNDERSTAND** why," Colette said. "If you can explain that to us, we might be able to figure out a way to help you."

Astro nodded solemnly. "It has to do with my *seven* cousins: Lunara, Celeste, Cosmia, Lyre, Pleadia, Maya, and Asteria," he began. "They are the **CREATORS** and **GUARDIANS** of harmony on Starlight."

"How do they do that?" Pam asked.

"They **DANCE**," Prince Astro replied. "Their dance is the fuel for the light nests that give **brightness** to the stars in our world. But

Celeste

Cosmia

Lunara

Lyre

now, the seven fairies have stopped **DANCING**."

"What happened?" Nicky asked.

A sad look crossed the prince's face.

"You see, there is another fairy; her name is Cometta, and her role is to be the master of harmony," Astro explained. "She is the one who gives **the dance rhythm** and teaches my cousins new steps. But Cometta has been missing for a long time."

Pleadia

Maya

Asteria

Cometta

"Oh no!" Violet exclaimed.

"Without a guide, my cousins have lost their ability to dance," Prince Astro continued. "There is no more *harmony* in the kingdom."

Will and the Thea Sisters were silent for a few moments after the prince finished his story.

Will broke the silence. "I imagine that you've **LOOKED** everywhere."

"Yes, but there has been no sign of her," Astro answered. "And each day, the light FADES more and more from our world."

"We will find her at any cost," Nicky promised.

"Yes, but *where* should we look?" Colette asked.

"Starlight is a **VAST** world," Paulina said, remembering the living map they had seen in headquarters.

"There is a way to find her, but it will be **DANGEROUS**," the prince said.

"We are willing to hear your plan," Will told him.

"I am so *grateful* to all of you," Prince Astro said. He took a deep breath. "I will explain to you what I think we can do."

The Thea Sisters **LOOKED** at one another and nodded. Then they exclaimed all together:

"We will always do whatever it takes to help you, *Prince Astro*!"

BRIGHTSTAR CASTLE

1. ENTRANCE
2. STARRY HEDGE
3. SILVER STAIRWAY
4. PRINCE ASTRO'S QUARTERS
5. THE APARTMENTS OF THE SEVEN FAIRY COUSINS
6. ROYAL HALL
7. COURT OF THE ARTS
8. SOUTH TOWER: APARTMENTS OF THE GOLD STAR FAIRIES
9. EAST TOWER: APARTMENTS OF THE SILVER STAR FAIRIES
10. WEST TOWER: APARTMENTS OF THE BLUE STAR FAIRIES
11. NORTH TOWER: APARTMENTS OF THE WHITE STAR FAIRIES
12. LIBRARY

THE FOUR
PEARLS OF LIGHT

Prince Astro rose from his throne, ready to begin explaining his plan.

"In the world of Starlight, there is an ancient legend about **FOUR PEARLS OF LIGHT** that are positioned on opposite ends of the map of the kingdom," he began. "They are capable of generating a ray of **starry light** that will show the way to any lost object. I believe we can use them to find Cometta."

"**Great!** Where can we find these pearls of light?" Nicky asked impatiently.

"The pearls, unfortunately, are kept in **_dangerous_** places that are difficult to reach. You must travel to the extreme ends of the kingdom and face clever guardians, who can be **CRUEL** and will make you pass various kinds of tests," Astro explained.

Paulina nodded and then spoke for everyone: "It won't be easy . . . but we will give it our all!"

"Then let me tell you where to find the pearls," Astro began. "The first pearl is in the Cloudy Peaks. They are rugged mountains that have been destroyed by UNPREDICTABLE space currents."

Cloudy Peaks

"That sounds pretty harsh," Pam remarked.

"That's not all, unfortunately," the prince continued. "The pearl is guarded by the winged BLUE SALAMANDER. She is very strong and clever."

"I guess she won't just give us the pearl, right?" Nicky asked.

"Obviously not, but legend says that the

salamander is very sensitive to the **melody** of an invisible **flute** called the moonstone flute, which can be found at the top of the Peak of Profound Sound, on the north side of the mountains," Astro replied.

"Are you serious? We have to play a flute for a flying lizard?" Pam asked.

"Salamander," Paulina corrected her. "But we're in luck. I play the flute!"

"Perfect!" Will said. He turned to Astro. "Where can we find the SECOND PEARL?"

"It's in the south, in a cave at the bottom of **Celestial Lake**," Astro responded. "It's a very UNUSUAL lake because there isn't water inside it. Instead, it's filled with clouds."

Celestial Lake

"That sounds very unusual," Paulina agreed.

"There is a village of celestial nymphs at the bottom, and they are very shy creatures," the prince went on. "If you manage not to **SCARE** them, they will lead you to where the pearl is kept."

"Where is the third pearl of light?" Colette asked.

"The third one is kept in the Cosmic Forest, a thick forest that is found in the west. But you can't cross through it alone," Astro said. "You need to find the Star Guide fairy."

"How will we recognize her?" Will asked.

Cosmic Forest

"She has green eyes and curly green hair, and she is very small," Astro answered. "To convince her to help you, once you've found her, you must solve —"

"Her **riddles**?" Nicky asked.

"Yes, how did you know?" the prince asked.

"Fairies love riddles," Nicky replied. "We already **solved** one of Sixtar's."

"If you solved that one, you can relax," Astro told her. "Sixtar is famous in all the kingdom for her difficult puzzles. I trust the Star Guide and you will reach the pearl."

"She will tell us where it is?" Paulina asked.

"We already know that the pearl is kept in the trunk of a thousand-year-old hollow tree," Astro said. "The guide will take you to it."

"And what about the fourth pearl?" Will asked.

"The fourth and last PEARL OF LIGHT is found on the PRIMAL ASTEROID," Astro replied.

"What a **MYSTERIOUS** name!" Paulina remarked.

"It's in the east. The asteroid was once the kingdom of the

Primal Asteroid

SILVER GOBLINS, who were creatures skilled in the art of forging the planet's rarest metals. But now it is a dry and deserted place. You can reach it by following an ancient bridge of light that extends through the **EMPTIEST** and **DEEPEST** space," Astro explained.

"That sounds way **worse** than playing the flute for a lizard," Pam said.

"Salamander," Nicky said.

"Whoever seeks the fourth pearl must be careful," the prince continued. "Guarding the pearl, **hidden** in dangerous silver quicksand, are the three **Silver Styxes**. They are winged creatures similar to large owls, marvelous and TERRIFYING at the same time."

"Okay, now they seem way, way worse than the salamander," Pam remarked.

"They are," Astro confirmed. "But as with the salamander, there is a way to tame them: Bring them a fragment of FIRE QUARTZ."

"What is that?" Will asked.

"It is a luminescent rock that can be found in the deepest crack in the asteroid, and the styxes can't get there because of their size," the prince answered. If you bring them a fragment of fire quartz, the styxes will fly you to where the pearl is. It is the only way to travel over the silver sand."

"We can do it!" Nicky said.

Will tapped his chin. "These are challenging tasks, and we need to accomplish them quickly."

"Should we split into groups?" Paulina asked.

Will nodded. "That's what I was thinking," he said. "Pam, Paulina, and I will get the pearls on the Cloudy Peaks and on the PRIMAL ASTEROID," he said. "Violet, Nicky, and Colette, you can head to Celestial Lake and the Cosmic Forest."

"Wait, we will get the BLUE lizard *and* the FLYING monsters?" Pam asked.

"Don't worry, Pam. We'll be in this together," Paulina said.

"I can't thank you enough," the prince said. "There are four bridges of light that leave from here. Following them you can reach north, east, west, and south. Good luck, friends. May you be successful on your mission!"

TOWARD THE
CLOUDY PEAKS

The team from the Seven Roses Unit left the castle.

"Agents, I won't hide the fact that I'm a bit worried about our mission," Will said. "It won't be easy to fᵢɴᴅ and RECOVER the four pearls of light. But if anyone can do it, it's you. You are some of the most capable and expert agents in the department."

Good luck!

Nicky smiled, and said, "Thanks, Will. You can be sure that we will give it our all!"

"Please do," Will warned.

"We will," Violet promised.

Meanwhile, the moment had arrived for the group to separate. The bridge of light that headed NORTH, which would lead Will, Paulina, and Pam toward the Cloudy Peaks, was in front of them.

Nicky, Colette, and Violet would head to the bridge to the south, the one that would take them to Celestial Lake.

"We will see you soon!" Pam said.

"Good luck!" Violet replied. The five friends *hugged* and got moving.

See you soon!

The mission in the Starlight Kingdom had officially begun. Will, Paulina, and Pam walked toward the Cloudy Peaks without speaking, focused on their objective.

After a while, Paulina was the one to break the silence. "Look! Those stars down there seem less bright than the others," she observed, pointing to her right.

"Cheese and crackers! You're right!" Pamela confirmed.

A dark look crossed Will's face. "This tells us that we need to move *FAST*, or the Starlight world will go dark forever."

"How FAR are the Cloudy Peaks from here?" Pam asked.

"Astro didn't say, but I'm guessing that we will soon be able to see them on the HORIZON," Will answered.

"I sure hope so," Pam said. "Although I'm not in too much of a *hurry* to meet that flute-loving lizard."

"Salamander," Paulina corrected her.

They continued along the *BRIDGE OF LIGHT* until they noticed something in front of them.

"There they are!" Pam exclaimed.

"Yes, those definitely look like the Cloudy Peaks," Paulina confirmed. Ahead of them, rough mountains of **STARRY QUARTZ** stood out imposingly beyond a blanket of white clouds. "This is good. We're getting closer to finding the first pearl!"

Keep close!

They moved quickly and reached the end of the *BRIDGE OF LIGHT*. As soon as they set foot on the light-colored rock, a strong wind struck them. They all huddled together. They tried to keep going, but the storm of ice and **stardust** made it **impossible** to see where they were going.

"These gusts of space wind are too strong," Pam said. "We'll never make it!"

"You're right," Paulina agreed. "We can't reach the top of the peaks under these conditions."

"Wait here for a moment," Will said. He pushed against the wind for several yards, and then returned. "There's a GORGE just up ahead. It's steep, but the rock walls on the two sides are a good SHELTER from the wind that's beating against the mountain."

"Okay," Pam agreed. "I like the idea of shelter."

"I'll lead the way," Will proposed. "But let's all keep our EYES OPEN. We don't exactly know where the BLUE SALAMANDER is. She could be anywhere!"

The three slowly began to climb the gorge,

grabbing the rocks with their paws and feet. Will was right — the gorge was STEEP — but there were enough rocks JUTTING OUT for them to grip. After a thirty-minute climb, they finally arrived, **EXHAUSTED**, but satisfied.

Pam flopped down on the rock platform. "Can we rest for a minute?" she asked. "That looks like a CAVE or something over there."

Paulina put a paw on her arm. "It sure does. And look what's sticking out of it!" she said in a loud whisper.

Jutting out of the cave was a **PAIR OF ENORMOUSE BLUE WINGS**!

THE MOONSTONE FLUTE

"That must be the lair of the BLUE SALAMANDER," Will said.

"Wait, I thought we were dealing with a regular-sized salamander," Pam said. "Those wings are **huge**!"

"Then I think we need to find the invisible flute as quickly as we can," Paulina said. "Then we can convince the Blue Salamander to give us the PEARL OF LIGHT, and get out of here."

"I like that idea," Pam said.

"Prince Astro said that the **Peak of Profound Sound** was in the north," Paulina remembered.

"And we came from the south, so we need to go along the side of the mountain," Will explained, and he immediately headed down a narrow path that ran along the side of the rock.

"Be careful, and try not to look **down**," Will warned.

"Holey cheese, I would never think about **looking down**!" Pamela exclaimed.

Then, suddenly, a thick cloud surrounded her and Paulina.

"I can't see anything!" Paulina cried. "Will? Pam? Where are you?"

Follow me!

Being careful to keep his balance, Will turned toward them, but he could only see clouds.

"Pamela, Paulina! Can you hear me?" he called.

"We're here, but we can't move forward!" Pam yelled.

"Stay calm, and I will **GUIDE YOU** with my voice," Will reassured them. "Keep one paw on the side of the rock. It will be your reference point."

"Done!" the two friends answered together.

"Good. Now continue putting one foot **SLOWLY** in front of the other," he instructed. "I am here, reach for my paw."

Pam and Paulina did as Will said, but it was challenging to move forward with no visibility, even for a short distance. But they persisted. After a few unending seconds,

Paulina finally saw something in front of her **Peeking** through the clouds: Will's paw! She grabbed it and he guided her out of the blanket of clouds.

She turned and called into the CLOUDS. "Pam, look for my paw now!" she instructed.

"Got it!" Pam replied, and a few seconds later, she grabbed Paulina's paw and stepped out of the clouds.

"Holey cheese, I'm glad we're finally out of that TERRIBLE FOG!" she remarked, breathing a sigh of relief.

"Let's keep going. We're close now," Will said, starting to walk again.

He was right. They went just a few more yards before they reached the NORTH side of the mountain. From there, it was easy to spot the highest **peak**.

"Do we need to climb up *there*?" Pam asked.

"I'm an expert climber," Will said. "I'll get the **flute** and bring it back so Paulina can play it."

Paulina and Pam nodded silently as Will began the **dangerous** climb to the top of the rocky peak.

"I hope he makes it up okay," Paulina said worriedly.

"He said he's an expert," Pam said. "If I know Will, he'll be fine. I'm just not sure how he's supposed to find the moonstone flute. I mean, it's invisible, right?"

Overhead, Will made his way to the top of the peak. When he reached the **summit**, he quickly looked around to assess the situation.

He had the same worry as Pam. How was he supposed to find something that was invisible?

He scanned the **ROCKY**

SURFACE inch by inch, and then a sparkle caught his eye. A beam of sunlight had struck a small, transparent object.

"The moonstone flute!" Will cried. He quickly grabbed it. As he removed it from the rock, some pieces of the peak broke off and rolled into the valley, hitting the sides of the mountain.

I found it!

Pam watched the rocks fall with big eyes, and a wave of dizziness swept over her. She quickly looked up.

"I will not

look down. I will not look down," she muttered.

"Careful, Will!" Paulina called out.

"I'm here!" Will replied. "I'm coming down with the flute."

But at that precise moment, a **SHARP CRY** rang out over the mountain peaks.

Paulina and Pam both felt their fur stand on end. A GIANT SHADOW darkened the sky. They looked up to see an **ENORMOUSE** creature flying overhead . . . the BLUE SALAMANDER!

THE FiRST PEARL
OF LiGHT

"Will, take cover!" Paulina yelled. "The Blue Salamander doesn't look very **friendly**!"

"We're out in the open here, too," Pam reminded her. "Let's look for shelter!"

They looked around, but there wasn't even a corner where they could **HiDE** out. A moment later, the monstrous creature nose-dived toward Paulina and Pam.

The salamander swooped past them without touching them, but the gust of air created by her huge wings almost sent them *TUMBLING* down the mountain. They had to clutch at the rocks to keep from falling.

"**HELP!**" Pam yelled.

"Hang on, Pam!" Paulina cried.

"**Aaaaiiiieeee!**" the salamander cried.

"Will, I need to play that flute to CALM DOWN the salamander!" Paulina called to him.

"Yeah, and you need to do it fast!" Pam added. "That BLUE BEAST is in a bad mood!"

"I can't climb down. The wind from the creature's wings is too strong," he called back. "If I throw it to you, can you catch it?"

"I think so," she replied. "But we need to time it just right."

"Aaaaiiiieeee!" the salamander shrieked. She swooped down again.

Paulina and Pam DUCKED and tried not to lose their balance. The creature SOARED up again, and the wind from her wings died down.

Paulina ran to the edge of the platform. "Ready, Will!" she yelled.

"On the count of three!" he called out. "One, two . . . three!"

Then he let go of the precious instrument. It fell from the top of the peak . . .

Paulina reached out and with one confident move grabbed the flute.

"**GOT IT!**" she cried, clutching it triumphantly in her hand.

"Nice job, Paulina!" Pam cheered.

Paulina turned to smile at her friend, but what she saw made her freeze in fright. The enormouse BLUE SALAMANDER was behind Pam, flying right toward her!

Pam noticed the look in Paulina's eyes.

"Uh-oh," she said, and she looked behind her. "Leaping lizards! I mean, simmering salamanders! There's nowhere to run!"

Paulina knew there was only one thing to do. She put the moonstone flute to her lips and closed her eyes. She tried to call up one of the MELODIES she knew so she wouldn't make a mistake.

She gently breathed into the flute and began to play. A VERY SWEET TUNE filled the air.

The Blue Salamander slowed down. She gently glided over to Paulina and perched on a nearby rock. Then her body began to sway to the music.

"Galloping gears, you did it!" Pam cheered over the sound of the tune. "You have tamed the BLUE BEAST!"

Will climbed down from the peak. "It would appear so," he said. "Now we just have to ask the Blue Salamander to give us the PEARL OF LIGHT."

Paulina, meanwhile, had not stopped playing the flute.

"Keep it up," Pam coached. "You're doing great!"

"We should approach the salamander while Paulina is playing the flute," Will suggested. "If she stops playing, the salamander might become AGGRESSIVE again."

Pam nodded. "I've got this!"

The salamander's eyes were closed as she lost herself in the music. Pam cautiously approached the creature. She could feel her heart pounding in her chest, but she knew she had to be **BRAVE**.

Pam quietly tiptoed up to the creature and whispered, "Kind Blue Salamander, we are here because we urgently need the pearl of light that you watch over. Prince Astro asks you to give it to us, for the good of the kingdom."

As soon as she stopped talking, the creature's eyes opened suddenly, making Pam JUMP. The giant creature stood up, opened her massive WINGS, and flapped them twice.

Pam had the strong sense that the salamander was communicating with them.

"I think she wants us to go with her," Pam said. She looked at the salamander. "Is that right?"

The creature nodded. Pam took a deep breath.

"Here we go," she muttered. She climbed onto the salamander's back. "Come on, guys."

Paulina climbed on, still playing the flute, and Will joined them. The salamander took off, flying around the mountain back to her nest at the bottom of the gorge. She gently landed and her passengers climbed off her back.

They followed the salamander into her cave. She nudged a pile of leaves aside to reveal a shiny, round object.

Here's the first pearl!

"It's the PEARL OF LIGHT!" Pam cried.

"I think she wants us to have it," Will said.

Pam grabbed it, and the salamander didn't stop her.

"Thank you so much, BLUE SALAMANDER," Pam said. "And now I guess we'll be going."

Paulina played the flute until they left the cave. Then she stopped and placed the instrument on top of a rock.

"We'd better start CLIMBING back down," Will said.

As they made their way down the mountain, they heard a sound coming from the cave. But it wasn't a *PIERCING* shriek. It was a deep, friendly roar.

"Rooowwwwwrrr!"

Pam smiled at Paulina. "I think she's thanking you," she said.

"How can you be sure?" Paulina asked.

"It's WEIRD," Pam replied. "I think I made a real connection with that salamander. Can you believe that?"

"This is a magical FAIRY WORLD where anything can happen," Paulina replied. "Of course I believe you!"

THE NYMPHS OF CELESTIAL LAKE

By the time Paulina, Pam, and Will had obtained the first PEARL OF LIGHT, Colette, Nicky, and Violet had made the long walk to the shores of Celestial Lake.

They stopped and stared into the lake, which was filled with clouds just as Prince Astro had described. "I've never seen a lake without water before," Nicky remarked.

"It is definitely very strange," Violet agreed.

Colette frowned. "Prince Astro said we need to travel to the nymphs who live in the bottom of the lake. But how do you move around in a lake filled with clouds? Do you swim? Do you fly?"

"We need to step in and see what happens!" Nicky replied.

She knelt down and CAUTIOUSLY put one foot into the lake. It disappeared into the FOGGY MASS.

"I can't feel anything solid on the bottom," she reported. "But my leg isn't SINKING. It's like the clouds are holding me up."

Nicky stood up. "I think maybe we can

Should we go in?

How does it work?

float on this stuff," she guessed. She put her other foot into the lake.

"It's strange," she tried to explain. "You go in but you don't go down because the cloud is dense. You should both try it so you can UNDERSTAND what I mean."

Colette stepped into the lake to see what Nicky was talking about.

"You're right," Colette remarked. "It really feels like walking on clouds!"

"Can this really be the way to get to the village of the nymphs?" Violet asked with suspicion in her voice.

"We need to have faith, Vi," Colette reassured her, taking her paw.

Violet followed Colette and Nicky into the lake. They started to WALK down, headed for the bottom.

As they got closer, they were able to see

structures through the clouds.

"This must be the village of the celestial nymphs!" Colette exclaimed.

"Let's approach slowly," Violet suggested. "We don't want to **SCARE** the nymphs."

The homes of the nymphs looked like bubbles. Yellow light glowed from inside. Fairies with blue wings flitted among the buildings.

One of the nymphs **SPOTTED** Colette, Nicky, and Violet. She pointed at the three friends and then ***darted*** inside her house. Startled, the other nymphs did the same thing.

"Oh no, we've **FRIGHTENED** them!" Violet said.

"Let's knock on some doors," Colette said.

They knocked on one door and asked for help, but the nymph inside did not open up. Neither did the nymph at the next house. At

the third house, Violet noticed a flower growing by the door.

"A moon flower!" she exclaimed.

The door opened up just a crack. A *melodic voice* spoke to them from inside.

"You know this flower?"

"I have seen a picture of it in my book of flowering plants," Violet answered. "I've never seen one in a garden before."

"So you know and love plants?" the nymph asked.

"Very much," Violet replied. "And the ones in your garden are really beautiful!"

The door opened wider, and a CELESTIAL NYMPH with long blue hair appeared.

"Who are you and why are you here?" she asked.

"My name is Violet, and together with my friends, we've come to save Starlight," Violet replied. "Your world is in **great danger**."

The nymph's blue eyes looked sad. "We know this to be true. But there is nothing to be done."

"Yes, there is!" Colette interrupted. "We are here to get the pearl of light that is kept in this lake, so we can use it to help your **WORLD**."

The nymph floated out of her house. One after another, other nymphs did too. Curious, they all gathered around the mouselets.

"The PEARL OF LIGHT isn't here in the village," one of the nymphs said.

"Then where is it?" Nicky asked.

"The pearl is kept in the cave of the **Moon Gnome**," another nymph replied.

"Is the cave in this lake?" Violet asked.

The nymph nodded. "It is, but I am **afraid**

that it won't be easy to get the pearl from him," she replied. "The gnome is extremely protective of his things."

"There must be a way to **CONVINCE** him," Nicky said.

The nymphs frowned thoughtfully. "We do not know the gnome very well. He isn't very social," one said. "But we can give you something that might help."

The other nymphs looked at her, confused. She disappeared into her house and returned with a round white B O X in her hand.

We can help you . . .

She opened the box, and a strong smell of pine and mint wafted through the air. "What is that?" Violet asked.

"It is a cream that we make from the vine of

the STARBERRY," the nymph replied. "You should put it under your **nose** before you enter the gnome's cave."

"Why do we need to do that?" Nicky asked.

"The gnome fills the entrance to his cave with star algae," the nymph answered. "It has a very **pungent** smell to keep out intruders."

Violet took the box from her. "Thank you! This will be very useful. How do we get to the cave?"

"You need to follow the white path on the east side of the village," another nymph explained. Stick to the path and you can't go wrong."

"We don't know how to thank you," Colette said.

"Go save Starlight!" all the nymphs cried out.

"We will do our best," the mouselets promised. Then they said good-bye to the nymphs and headed toward the cave.

WHAT A STENCH!

Colette, Nicky, and Violet easily found the **WHITE PATH** and hurried along it, looking for the cave of the Moon Gnome.

"It's a good thing you recognized that moon flower, Violet," Nicky told her. "The nymphs might not have helped us otherwise!"

"I think it's going to be a lot harder to convince the **Moon Gnome** to help us," Violet said.

They reached the end of the path. In front of them was the opening of a **CAVE** in the wall of the lake.

"This must be the gnome's house," Violet guessed.

Nicky sniffed the air. "Whoa! You can smell the **stench** from here. It's worse than rotten cheese!"

Colette nodded. "It's awful!" She put her **PAW** in front of her nose.

Violet opened up the **BOX** that the nymphs had given them. She rubbed some of the cream under her nose, as they had instructed. She breathed in the clean, fresh smell.

"Here," she said, holding out the box to her friends who applied the cream.

"It works!" Colette cried. "All I can smell now is pine and mint."

"No more **stinky stench**," Nicky remarked.

Violet nodded. "I think we should go in."

They entered the cave. Soft YELLOW light filtered in through some cracks in the cave's rock walls. Under their feet, something SQUISHED as they walked.

"This must be the **ALGAE** that the nymphs told us about," Nicky remarked. "Algae's a plant, right?"

"Right," Violet said. "Seaweed is a type of algae. I'm not sure what this is, but it's so MUSHY! It's like walking in sludge."

"Thank goodness the nymphs gave us this cream," Colette added.

They reached a room in the cave lit up by a giant candle that dripped wax onto the floor. They could see a spiral slide on the other side of the room, and an unusual giant game board on the floor.

"This place is creepy," Colette said with a shiver.

As soon as she spoke, someone SLID down the slide and landed on the floor in front of them.

Nicky gasped. "It's the Moon Gnome!"

THE WINNING MOVE

The gnome was very small. He had a long gray beard and wore white robes and a dome-shaped hat on his head. He didn't speak, but he stared at them with his cold gray eyes.

Nicky spoke up. "Good day, Mr. Gnome. We are here for a very *important* reason."

The gnome continued to stare at them.

"We come in the name of **Prince Astro**," Violet added. "He has asked us to bring him the PEARL OF LIGHT."

"The Starlight Kingdom is in danger," Colette concluded. "In order to help the **kingdom**, we must have the pearl."

Finally, the gnome spoke. "Finished, have you?"

"Yes," Violet replied.

The gnome laughed so hard that his voice *echoed* throughout the cave.

"This isn't funny!" Colette said, irritated. "This situation is very serious!"

The gnome *snickered* even harder, nearly keeling over from all the laughter.

"The stars of Starlight will go out for good if we don't do something," Violet said. But the gnome kept **laughing**.

"Okay, enough. What do you want in exchange for the pearl?" Colette burst out.

The gnome **immediately** stopped laughing.

"Finally, you have asked the right question!" he said.

"So, what do you want?" Colette

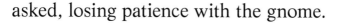

asked, losing patience with the gnome.

"To play," he answered simply.

"Play what?" Colette asked, surprised.

He pointed to a big game board on the floor.

"Move, you do; move, I do," the gnome responded.

"Really? You want to play a game to decide the fate of your world?" Violet asked.

"Move, you do; move, I do," the gnome repeated, leaving no room for doubt. "If you WIN, yours the pearl is."

Violet looked at Colette and Nicky. "What should we do?"

"I don't think we have a **choice**," Nicky replied. "We need to play him."

"I'm sure he's very good at this game," Colette guessed. "He seems CONFIDENT that he can beat us. But we have to try!"

Colette turned to the Moon Gnome. "We accept your challenge. But you need to give us your word that if we **WIN**, we will get the pearl."

"I promise," he responded.

Colette walked around the game board, studying it. On one side of the board were game pieces shaped like spheres. On the other side, the game pieces were G R A Y C U B E S .

"The rules I will give," the gnome said. "The pieces only move diagonally. If an opponent's piece it meets, gobble it, it can, if free is the next space. Whoever has more pieces on the opposite side gets, **WINS**. Easy."

We need to beat him!

"It's almost like a game of **CHECKERS**," Violet observed.

"Let's begin!" the gnome said impatiently. "Your turn!"

"We can do this," Violet whispered to Colette and Nicky. "We've played enough **CHECKERS** on game night at Mouseford!"

Her friends nodded. Violet pointed to one of the spheres. "Move that one **there**," she said, pointing to a square.

They rolled the sphere diagonally onto an empty space. Then the gnome moved one of his **CUBES**. They each took another turn.

Violet scanned the board. "That cube has

Great move!

A point for us!

a free space in front of it. We can **capture** it!"

They rolled a sphere onto a space with one of the cubes. The sphere **magically** gobbled up the cube!

"How dare you?" the gnome shrieked.

"We just followed the rules of the game," she replied. "Your rules."

He frowned. "Fine. continue, we will!"

They took turns. Then Nicky rolled one of the spheres onto a space with one of the

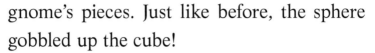

gnome's pieces. Just like before, the sphere gobbled up the cube!

Furious, the gnome began to walk in circles, HUFFING and puffing.

"Unfair, this is!" he wailed.

"We are playing fair and square," Violet told him, and the gnome couldn't argue.

"He's losing the game," Colette whispered.

The gnome stroked his beard, trying to regain his concentration. Then he broke into a grin.

"Turn the tide, I will!" he said, and he pushed one of his cubes onto a square with a sphere. For the first time, one of his cubes **DEVOURED** a sphere!

"Uh-oh, he's catching up," Colette said. "What should our next move be?"

"Don't worry, I think I've got this," Violet said. "You just need to look at the board

LOGICALLY, and think a few steps ahead."

The mouselets made a move. Then the gnome. Then the mouselets. Then the gnome. One by one, the spheres gobbled up the cubes.

Finally, there was just one cube left on the board, and four spheres.

"**IMPOSSIBLE**, this is!" the gnome cried.

"Actually, it's very possible," Violet said. They pushed the sphere onto the final cube's space. The last cube DISAPPEARED.

"We win!" Nicky cheered.

"Possible it isn't! Possible it isn't!" he continued to repeat, pacing back and forth.

The mouselets hugged one another.

"Good job, Violet," Nicky said. "You're a real **ACE** at checkers!"

Violet grinned. "Thanks! I'm just glad I could help."

"Now you must keep your promise and

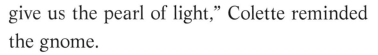
give us the pearl of light," Colette reminded the gnome.

Without saying a word, he TOOK OFF his hat, revealing a glowing pearl underneath, balancing on the top of his head. He gave it to the mouselets with a sigh.

"Very good, you were," he said.

"Thank you, we do," Nicky said with a smile.

"If you wouldn't mind ONE MORE question," Violet said, "Can you please tell us how to get to the Cosmic Forest?

"West, you must go," the gnome answered. Then he walked over to the spiral slide and somehow slid *up* and away, out of sight.

IN THE THICK OF THE COSMIC FOREST

Violet, Colette, and Nicky left the cave and headed WEST until they reached another BRIDGE OF LIGHT.

"This way to the Cosmic Forest!" Nicky cried happily as they crossed the bridge.

"I have to admit, facing that Moon Gnome wasn't as bad as I thought it might be," Violet said.

"That's because you're great at checkers!" Colette said. "And I'm glad you are, because now we have one of the PEARLS OF LIGHT! We just need to get one more."

Violet was thoughtful. "What was it that Prince Astro said? We can't get through the forest without a guide."

"He said to look for the Star Guide fairy,"

Colette added. "And that she was very small."

"He also said that we will have to

More riddles... solve some **riddles**!" Nicky reminded them. She sighed. "More riddles. I sure wish PAULINA were with us. She's great at solving riddles."

The mouselets went **silent**, thinking of their friends who were far away, searching for the other two pearls.

"I hope they are **safe**," Violet said.

"I'm sure they are," Nicky assured her.

"We can't let them down," Colette said. "We'll do our best to answer the riddles of the Star Guide. Between the three of us, I'm sure we can!"

They came to the end of the bridge and stepped onto a new **planet**. In front of them, tall trees twisted high into the night sky. Leaves that looked like stars SHONE on their branches.

"This must be the Cosmic Forest!" Nicky said.

Violet gazed up at the STARRY leaves. "Wow, it's beautiful!"

"But this planet is thick with trees," Nicky said. "How are we supposed to find a tiny fairy here? It will be like finding a needle in a HAYSTACK."

"Let's think positively," Colette said. "Maybe the fairy will find us. Who knows?"

The three friends stepped into the forest. The ground felt SOFT underneath their feet. As they walked deeper into the forest, they saw that the starry leaves came in all different colors: PINK, BLUE, ORANGE, GREEN, YELLOW, and more.

"This is no ordinary forest," Nicky said.

"It's a **rainbow of colors**!" Violet agreed.

"It's so beautiful here," Colette said. She turned in a circle, looking up at the colorful, **glowing** canopy of leaves overhead. Without thinking about it, she began to sing.

Nicky and Violet recognized the SONG and joined in. The sound of the **HAPPY TUNE** rang through the forest.

As they sang, a tiny fairy flew out of the leaves.

"Hello!" she called out in a musical voice.

Hello!

She had **green** eyes and a crown of golden stars in her curly **green** hair.

"Hello," the three friends replied.

"I am the Star Guide fairy," she said. "I heard your lovely song and it gave me great **JOY**, as does your presence here. We never get visitors in this forest."

"I'm sorry to hear that," Violet said. "Your forest is BEAUTIFUL!"

The fairy smiled, pleased. "Thank you," she said.

"There is a reason why we came here," Colette said. "**Prince Astro** sent us. We need to ask you for your PEARL OF LIGHT so that we can save the Starlight Kingdom."

The fairy's sweet face turned serious. "I can show you where the pearl is, but first you must correctly answer my riddles," she said. "It is the rule of the forest."

"Yes, the prince told us," Colette replied.

"Then let us begin," the Star Guide said.

The three friends focused, ready for their new challenge . . .

THE RIDDLES OF THE STAR GUIDE

"Pay *close attention* now," the Star Guide fairy began. She stared at an ORANGE star-shaped leaf on a nearby branch. The leaf fell off and hovered in the air in front of them.

"Is that writing on the leaf?" Colette asked.

"It's the riddle!" Nicky cried.

Violet PLUCKED the leaf out of the air and began to read out loud.

"When it's HOT, it gets dressed," Violet began.

"And when it's cold, it undresses," Colette finished. "What is it?"

"The answer must

When it's hot, it gets dressed. When it's cold it undresses. What is it?

be something that does the **opposite** of what you would usually do," Violet mused.

The friends were quiet for a minute, PONDERING the answer. Nicky looked up, gazing at the leaves overhead, when the answer came to her.

"I've got it! It's a tree!" she cried. "In the winter it loses its leaves — just like taking off a coat, or undressing. And in the summer, when it's hot out, it gets dressed with LEAVES again!"

She looked at the fairy, hoping she was right. The Star Guide smiled.

"Correct! You have guessed the first answer. Well done!" she congratulated Nicky. "But I still have two more riddles for you."

The Star Guide fairy made another *movement* with her hand and once again a **STAR-SHAPED** leaf floated down toward them. This leaf was blue, with the SECOND RIDDLE written on it.

If you have one, you want to say it. But if you say it, you don't have it anymore. What is it?

"Let's put our heads together," Violet said. "What is something you want to say?"

"Hmm. Good news?" Nicky guessed.

"You don't lose **GOOD NEWS** once you tell it," Violet pointed out.

Colette looked **THOUGHTFUL**. "What about GOSSiP? I always want to say it as soon as I hear it."

Violet's face brightened. "That's close, Colette. But it's not quite it. I think I know."

She turned to the Star Guide fairy. "Is it a

secret? Once you tell it, you don't have it anymore."

"Correct!" the fairy replied. "Answer one more riddle, and I can take you to the pearl of light."

She waved her hand one last time, and a **PINK** leaf floated down to the mouselets.

"What listens but doesn't talk?" Colette wondered.

"Maybe it's the wind," Nicky speculated.

"I'm not so sure about that,"

It always listens to everything, but it never says a word. What is it?

Violet said. "The wind whispers. Maybe it's an animal?"

The fairy shook her head. "You have one more guess. If you are wrong, you lose the pearl."

"**Let's think** carefully before we respond," Nicky urged.

They were all quiet for a minute.

"So quiet," Colette said, and then her eyes got wide. "I think I know. We listen with our **EARS**, and they can't talk back!"

"Brilliant, Colette!" Violet cried.

Colette turned to the fairy. "We've got it! The answer is the ear!"

The Star Guide *clapped* her hands. "You guessed it! Good, now I can take you to the pearl of light.

Colette, Nicky, and Violet hugged one another triumphantly.

THEY HAD DONE IT!

"You were very kind," Violet said to the fairy.

"It was a pleasure! But now **LET'S HURRY**. Soon the wind will pick up and it could be harder to get the pearl," she explained.

"Why is that?" Nicky wanted to know.

"You will find out when you see where it is," the fairy answered. "Follow me!"

She headed into the thick of the *forest*, skillfully weaving through the branches of the trees.

Follow me!

THE THOUSAND-YEAR-OLD TREE

The three Thea Sisters followed the Star Guide fairy into the crowded **Cosmic Forest**, marveling at how she guided them through that tangle of branches and leaves. They walked for a long time with the fairy **flying** in front of them, turning back every once in a while to make sure the mouselets were still there.

Finally, the little fairy announced, "We are almost there. The place is just beyond those trees!"

The mouselets followed her, pushing aside the **starry** foliage until, to their surprise, they found themselves in a clearing. Rising up from the forest floor was a **giant tree** without any leaves. The tree was larger than

any of the other trees in the forest, with **KNOTTY** and twisted roots.

"This must be a very **ancient** tree," Nicky guessed.

"That's true," the fairy replied. "This is the oldest tree in the **KINGDOM**."

"I imagine, though, that it wasn't always so bare," Colette said.

The Star Guide shook her head. "No, it wasn't," she replied. "It was once a **tree** like the others, dressed in splendid starry leaves. But one night there was a very violent cosmic storm that uprooted all the trees in the forest. This was the only tree that survived, but its leaves didn't."

"But the trees in the forest now — they grew after the storm?" Violet asked.

"Yes, all these trees are very young," the fairy answered. "This old tree watches over them, sharing its *wisdom* with them."

"What a wonderful old tree, to watch over other trees and guard the pearl of light," Nicky said.

Violet looked up at the twisted, bare branches. "Where is the pearl?"

The fairy pointed to the tree's massive trunk. "It is in there," she said. "The tree is hollow. You must climb *up* to the top, and then climb DOWN into the trunk."

Violet looked worried. "Up there?"

"I'm afraid there's no other way," the fairy explained.

"It's okay. I'LL GO!" Nicky offered.

"Are you sure?" Colette asked.

"Violet's good at checkers, and I'm good at rock *climbing*," she said. "This won't be too different than scaling a rock wall."

She approached the trunk and began her

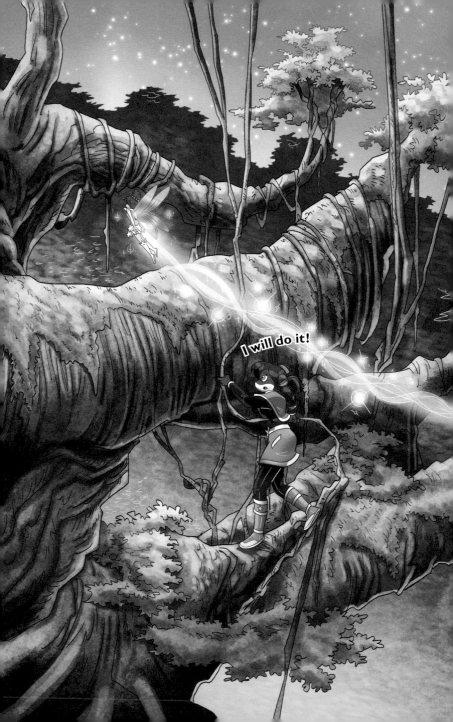

climb, grasping pieces of thick, **gnarled** bark.

An **EXPERT** climber, she quickly made her way up to the trunk of the tree. She had help from the Star Guide fairy, who flew alongside her and gave her advice.

"Move your paw to the right! There's a **STURDY** piece of bark there!"

With one last burst of effort, Nicky pulled herself up to the **highest** part of the trunk. She stopped to rest for a moment, and then she peered down into the hollow of the tree and saw something **glimmering** in the darkness below.

"The pearl is down there!" she called out to her friends. "I see a light coming out of it!"

"Yes, that is the pearl," the Star Guide confirmed.

"Do you think you can **reach** it?" Violet asked.

"I'll try to climb down," Nicky answered.

"**I'M SORRY** I can't help you," the Star Fairy said. "I'm too small to carry the pearl."

"You've already done a lot, kind fairy. Don't worry," Nicky assured her.

She stepped down into the trunk of the tree, testing the inside of the **WOOD** with her foot. It felt sturdy. She stepped in and then saw a long, **THICK VINE** growing down the inside of the trunk.

"Perfect!" she said. She grabbed ahold of the vine and began to shimmy down. The trunk smelled **PLEASANTLY** of old wood and moss.

She reached the pearl, a round orb that glowed with a soft light from within. She knew she needed both paws for the climb back up, so she untied the uniform **CAPE** from around her neck. She wrapped the pearl in it

carefully and attached it to her belt.

"Got it!" she called to her friends on the outside. "I'm coming back up."

"Be careful!" Colette advised.

Nicky began to climb very **carefully**, making sure not to damage the old tree in any way. When she reached the top of the trunk, she sat on a branch and unwrapped the pearl to show her friends.

"Hooray!" Violet and Colette cheered.

Victory! **VICTORY!**

VICTORY! *Victory!*

VICTORY!

THE PRIMAL ASTEROID

Meanwhile, on the **OPPOSITE** end of the kingdom, Will, Paulina, and Pamela finally had the PRIMAL ASTEROID in their sights. Now they were on a *BRIDGE OF LIGHT* leading to the deepest, darkest portion of Starlight.

"It's pretty **SPOOKY** out here," Pam said. "The perfect habitat for creepy creatures called the **Silver Styxes**, I'm guessing."

"Maybe they won't be so creepy," Paulina said. "After all, you ended up bonding with the BLUE SALAMANDER."

"True," Pam said. "I'll keep an open mind until I meet them."

Will, meanwhile, was looking into the **DISTANCE** and frowning.

"That's strange," he said.

"Can you be more specific? Everything is STRANGE out here," Pam said.

"Look at the last piece of the bridge up ahead of us," Will said. "It appears to be shaking. As though it's unstable."

At that moment, a sudden gust of wind made the whole bridge tremble.

"Help!" Paulina yelled. Underneath her feet, a piece of the bridge had actually broken off! She jumped back onto the solid part of the bridge, and Pam grabbed her arm as she flew.

"That was SCARY," Paulina said. "You're right, Will. This bridge is not stable!"

"We need to proceed with CAUTION from now on," Will said, looking around.

They moved ahead slowly. The bridge kept shaking, and big chunks of it were missing!

Finally, they spotted a cold GRAY object in the sky up ahead.

"That must be the PRIMAL ASTEROID," Pam guessed. "It looks abandoned."

"I have a FEELING that this path we're on isn't used very often," Paulina observed. "You're right, Pam. It doesn't look like there's any LIFE on that asteroid."

"Except for the three enormouse, FIERCE predators that Prince Astro warned us about," Pam reminded her.

"How could I forget?" Paulina replied with a smile.

Will looked down at the bridge. "This bridge seems to be weakening quickly. I hope we can find a different bridge when we leave the asteroid."

"*If* we leave the asteroid," Pam said.

"Don't say that, Pam," Paulina said, but

she was starting to become just as **nervous**.

The bridge ended, and they stepped onto the surface of the asteroid.

"Cheese niblets, what a deserted place!" Pam said. "And it's cold, too."

"Prince Astro said that the styxes will take us to the pearl if we give them a **FIRE QUARTZ** from deep in the belly of the asteroid," Paulina said. "But how will we get there?"

"We don't have specific directions, so we will have to **explore**," Will concluded.

Before they got far, they heard some **PIERCING SCREAMS** in the sky that made their blood freeze.

"**EEEEEEEEEEEEEEE!**"

"Uh-oh. That has to be the **Silver Styxes**," Pam said. "And they don't sound happy."

"RUN FOR COVER!" Will instructed, and the three of them tore across the rocky ground. Will headed for a large boulder not far away.

"EEEEEEEEEEEEEEE!"

"They're getting closer!" Paulina yelled.

Luckily, they reached the boulder and hid before the **Silver Styxes** found them. Breathless, they looked up in the sky to see the three creatures *circling* overhead.

There was a depression behind the boulder, and all three of them fit inside it. But the styxes SPOTTED them, and they kept diving down, trying to reach their prey.

"Get away from us!" Pamela yelled, but the styxes did not back down.

"We're trapped!" Paulina cried.

SAVE YOURSELF!

"EEEEEEEEEEEEE!" the styxes shrieked. They swiped at the three mice with their sharp talons. The mice ducked.

"Good-bye, Starlight!" Pam said. "Looks like we are about to be **STYX SNACKS**!"

Then Paulina noticed something — a large opening in the boulder. It seemed to lead to an **underground** tunnel!

"I think I see a way out of here," she said, pointing. "But we don't know where it leads. It's too **DARK** to see what's in there."

"As long as there are no **Silver Styxes** in there, we should be fine," Pam said.

"What do you think, Will?" Paulina asked.

"EEEEEEEEEEEEEEE!"

"Um, can we make a decision, please?" Pam asked anxiously.

I'll try to go in!

"I don't think we have a **CHOICE**," Will said. "This tunnel may be our only **HOPE**."

"I'll go first!" Pam offered.

"Okay, but be careful," Will warned.

"You got it," Pam said. She stuck her head inside the opening. She wiggled, and her shoulders fit through next.

She popped back out. "It's **NARROW**, but I think we can get through," she said.

"**EEEEEEEEEEEE!**" Another styx dove, and his **TALONS** brushed against Will's fur.

"Hurry, Pam!" Will urged.

He and Paulina watched Pam squeeze through the crack in the boulder. Suddenly, they heard her cry out.

"Holey cheese!"

Will and Paulina PEERED through the opening. They saw Pam standing with her back up against the wall of the tunnel, with a surprised and FRIGHTENED look on her face.

"What's happening?" Will asked. "Are you okay?"

"You need to come down here and see this!" Pam responded.

Paulina squeezed through the opening. Will kept an eye on the styxes, and when she was safely inside, he followed her in.

It took a second for his eyes to adjust to the darkness, and then . . .

HE LOOKED AROUND AND UNDERSTOOD WHY PAMELA WAS SO SHOCKED.

Below them was a giant cave that went

deep into the heart of the asteroid.

But the most surprising thing was that at the bottom of the cave, there appeared to be an enormouse underground city. It looked incredibly ancient. All around, set in the walls of the rock, they could see the remains of structures that looked like houses, workshops, and warehouses, linked by terracing and TUNNELS.

Time had destroyed nearly everything, and the little that remained was covered by a layer of gray dust that looked like ash.

"Cheese niblets, what a place!" Pam exclaimed. "This must be the village of the Silver Goblins that Prince Astro told us about, remember?"

"I remember," Paulina said. "That means that the FIRE QUARTZ should be down there somewhere."

Will looked around and saw a stairway that **WOUND** around the whole inside of the cave.

"I think that will get us down there," he said.

"It looks very narrow," Paulina remarked.

"We have to be very careful," Will said. "Follow me."

And he led the way toward the

GHOST CITY.

THE FIRE QUARTZ

Paulina, Pam, and Will moved in single file along the ledge of rock, being careful with every step. Will's foot hit a small rock that rolled off the ledge and fell down to the bottom of the cave. They all watched it fall.

Pam gulped. "Galloping gears, that's deep!"

"At least the styxes can't follow us in here," Paulina remarked.

"That's a relief!" Pam agreed.

"I'm pretty excited, actually," Paulina said. "We are taking an amazing journey to the center of the asteroid. But where will we end up?"

Pam looked down, and her eyes widened. "Hey, I think I see something sparkling down there!"

Something's sparkling!

Paulina squinted down into the depths. "I see it, too!" she cried. "Maybe it's the FIRE QUARTZ we are looking for!"

They traveled the rest of the way without speaking. When they reached the bottom of the cavern, they found themselves facing a tall, sparkling block of red crystal that gave off a fiery shimmer.

Pam reached out with her paw and then quickly pulled it back. "There's heat coming off of it!" she said. "This has to be the FIRE QUARTZ!"

They all stared at the giant crystal for a moment. The stone seemed to be alive, **PULSING** with red energy.

"It's **hypnotizing**," Paulina whispered. "But it's so big! There's no way we can get it out of this cavern to bring it to the styxes."

The three of them stared at the CRYSTAL in silence, without really knowing what to do. Then Pam's eyes got wide.

"I think I see something!" she said, and she *hurried* to a corner of the cave and reached down. Then she turned back to them with a glittering piece of the FIRE QUARTZ in her paw.

"This must have broken off of the main stone!" she said. "We're **IN LUCK**!"

"Good thing you spotted it!" Paulina said.

Pam tucked the piece of fire quartz into a pocket on her uniform.

"Well done, Pam!" Will exclaimed happily. "Let's go back up to the surface now. The

Silver Styxes are waiting for us."

"That's what I'm **AFRAID** of," Pam joked.

"If what Prince Astro said is true, then we can **TAME** them with the fire quartz," Paulina said. "I can't wait to see what happens!"

Paulina led the way as they **CAREFULLY** came out of the cavern to the tunnel that would lead back outside. It was a tiresome journey, but less scary than the way down.

When they arrived at the crack in the boulder, Paulina peeked outside. A **dark shadow** flew overhead.

"The styxes are still here!" she cried. She quickly ducked back inside as one of the creatures' talons reached for her. Outside they could hear the chilling **SHRIEKS** of the three large predators.

We have the quartz!

"What should we do?" Pam asked. "They're going to SCOOP us up!"

"I will go first," Will said. He held out his paw. "Pam, give me the quartz. Maybe they will CALM DOWN when they see it."

She took it out of her pocket and handed it to him.

Will climbed out of the opening, holding the FIRE QUARTZ in front of him. Paulina and Pam followed him.

As soon as the styxes set their eyes on the fire quartz, they suddenly stopped as if under a spell. They calmly landed on the ground.

Will took a few steps toward them. "Silver Styxes, we are here to save the marvemouse world of Starlight."

The three creatures BLINKED at him, waiting to hear more.

"It's working!" Paulina whispered to Pam.

"We need your help," Will continued. "We need to get the pearl of light that is in the silver sand. We bring you this fire quartz as a sign of our **good intentions**."

Will slowly set the fire quartz down in front of the styxes. Then he backed away and waited with Paulina and Pam.

After what felt like **FOREVER**, one of the monsters took the fragment in his beak and flew off, followed by the others.

We need the pearl of light!

"Do you think they will **COME BACK**?" Paulina wondered. "They never actually made an agreement to help us."

"Prince Astro said they would help," Will said. "I'm going to have faith."

They waited hopefully, and a few minutes later, the shiny silver of the styxes sparkled once more on the horizon.

"There they are!" Pam cried happily.

"But there are only **TWO** of them," Paulina observed, confused.

The two styxes landed on the **ROCKS** in front of them, and that's when the mice noticed a MYSTERIOUS figure riding on the back of one of the creatures.

"Who is that?" Pam whispered.

"I have no idea," Paulina replied.

The figure climbed off the styx and strode toward them, wearing a **DARK** cape and a hood that covered his head. When he reached them, he lowered his head to reveal a young face with sparkling silver eyes.

"My name is **Caliman**, and I am the lord of the Silver Goblins," he began. "We are a very hard-working community: We forge **METALS** mined from the insides of stars, and we distribute them throughout the kingdom. We were nomadic for some time, but when we reached this **asteroid**, the richness of the silver mines here convinced us to stay."

"Is that why you built your VILLAGE here?" Pamela asked.

"Exactly," Caliman replied. "But we should have listened to the prophecy."

"When we arrived here, we found a warning engraved in stone," he replied. "*Whoever invades this place, no matter how noble his ideals, will sprout wings after one hundred* **full moons** *have lit up the sky. Only a fiery quartz gathered by a fearless stranger can bring you back to your original form."*

"We didn't believe the warning, and we stayed here too long," Caliman said. "But you broke the SPeLL that transformed us into styxes. With this fire quartz fragment, I can finally free my people. I am in your debt."

"We are happy that we could help you," Will replied. "You can repay us by taking us to the PEARL OF LIGHT."

"We will be happy to help you with this **BOLD** undertaking," the lord of the goblins answered. "I admire your COURAGE and hope you are successful."

He motioned to the two giant birds. "These are two of my most trusted **knights**. They will lead you to the pearl."

The two styxes lowered their heads to invite the three mice to climb aboard. Then they opened their MASSIVE WINGS and lifted off in flight.

"The Primal Asteroid looks even more dry and deserted from up here," Pam remarked.

But a few minutes later, they flew over an area that sparkled.

"It's the silver sand!" Paulina cried. "How beautiful!"

Will gazed down. "I think I see something down there that is SHIMMERING brighter than the sand," he said, pointing.

"It could be the PEARL OF LIGHT," Pam said hopefully.

The two styxes began to fly downward.

"You must be right," Pam said. "It looks like they're taking us right to it!"

The styx dove down, right above the sand,

It's down there!

and then suddenly veered back up after brushing against the surface.

"What just happened?" Pam called out.

"He got the **PEARL OF LIGHT**!" Paulina answered her. "He has it in his claws."

"Great!" Pam replied.

The two styxes flew away from the silver sand, and soon landed at the base of a new BRIDGE OF LIGHT. Paulina, Pam, and Will climbed off the backs of the giant birds.

The styx who was holding the PEARL dropped it from his claws right next to them. Then the two creatures left in SILENCE, disappearing in the GRAY sky.

TOGETHER AGAIN!

After saying good-bye and thanking the Star Guide fairy, Nicky, Colette, and Violet reached the **BRIDGE OF LIGHT** that led back to **BRIGHTSTAR CASTLE**.

"Even though we got the two pearls, this mission is far from over," Nicky observed as she went along.

"It's true," Violet agreed. "Now we need to use the **PEARL OF LIGHT** to find **Cometta**."

"I hope that our friends found the other two **PEARLS OF LIGHT** so that we can start to search for her," Colette said.

She didn't know it, but Pamela, Will, and Paulina had succeeded in getting the pearls of light from the **Cloudy Peaks** and the **PRIMAL ASTEROID**. And at that same moment, they were also heading back to Brightstar Castle.

"I really hope that Colette, Violet, and Nicky *found* their pearls of light," Paulina remarked. "And more than that, I hope they're safe!"

"I'm sure they are," Will said. "Maybe they've already arrived at the castle and are waiting for us."

The thought of seeing their friends soon cheered up Paulina and Pam as they took the long, long walk over the bridge.

"This is the longest one," Pam remarked. "I don't think it's ever going to end!"

Suddenly, Paulina's eyes got wide. "Look up ahead. Is that them?"

In the distance, they could make out three figures silhouetted against the starry sky.

"I think so!" Pam replied. She cupped her paws around her mouth and yelled, "THEAAAAAAA SISTERRRRRRRRS!"

Up ahead, Colette stopped. "Did you *hear* that?" she asked Violet and Nicky.

The three friends turned around — and saw Paulina, Pam, and Will far behind them.

"It's them!" Nicky cried. She burst into a **run**, and Colette and Violet followed her. When they reached one another, they all **HAPPILY** hugged.

Together again!

"Did you get the pearls?" Pam asked.

"We did!" Colette and Violet cried, showing off the **PEARLS OF LIGHT** that they had found.

"**WELL DONE**, agents. I am really proud of you," Will said.

"And you?" Nicky asked.

"We almost got devoured by a giant **BLUE LIZARD** and three **monster birds**, but we did it," Pam replied.

"I'm glad you didn't get eaten," Violet said.

"Me, too," Pam agreed.

"But the best thing is that we're all together again," Paulina said. "We've got the four pearls, and I know we will be able to find Cometta and **SAVE** this kingdom."

"**HURRAY FOR THEA SISTERS!**" Colette exclaimed.

"Hurray!" the others joined in.

"Let's go find Prince Astro," Will said, **gazing** up ahead at Brightstar Castle. "We have four bits of **good news** to give him."

"He is going to be so **happy** when he sees the pearls!" Nicky added.

The group reached the entrance of the **palace** and stopped for a moment to admire the marvemouse structure that jutted out toward the sky.

"Am I wrong or is there **less light** here than when we left?" Paulina asked.

"The stars are definitely less bright," Colette answered. "We have no time to lose!"

She knocked on the **golden door**, which was answered by a fairy of the stars. Recognizing them, she smiled warmly.

"Welcome back," she said. "I'm happy to see you. *Prince Astro* asked me to greet you and take you to him when you arrived. Please, follow me."

"Thank you, **kind** fairy," Will answered.

The five mice followed the **fairy** down the halls of the castle until they reached Prince Astro's **throne** room. He was seated on top of his throne, lost in **thought** with his chin in his hands.

"Prince Astro, we've returned!" Will announced.

The prince **jumped to his feet** and went to meet them.

What a joy to see you!

"Dear friends, what a **JOY** to see you and know that you're well," he greeted them.

"We did our best to complete our tasks and

return to the palace as quickly as possible," Will told him.

"Were your TASKS successful?" Astro inquired.

"Yes," Will responded, **signaling** to the others. Colette, Violet, Pam, and Paulina stepped forward, holding the four pearls of light.

The prince's eyes got wide. "You have done it!" he said. "What **BRAVE** strangers you are, to risk your safety just to help the Starlight Kingdom. I thank you from the bottom of my *heart*."

"We're happy to help you, but we aren't done yet," Colette said. "How can we use the pearls to find out where Cometta is?"

The prince nodded. "**Follow me**," he said.

THE MAP OF THE KINGDOM

As they followed Prince Astro down the wide corridors of Brightstar Castle, Will and the Thea Sisters **noticed** that there was a strange atmosphere in the palace. Everything seemed like it was **suspended** in air in an unnatural silence.

"What's happening here at the castle, Prince Astro?" Colette asked, **WORRIED**. "There aren't any fairies around, and everything is **DARKER** and sadder than it was when we left."

Astro nodded and his eyes suddenly got sad.

"Unfortunately, my seven cousins are sadder and sadder, and the whole court feels it," he replied. "As you know, they have not been able to *dance* ever since Cometta disappeared."

Colette nodded. "And because they can't dance, the stars are **LOSING** their light."

"Exactly," the prince replied. "The stars are getting **fainter** and **colder**, and that is affecting the harmony of the kingdom. Fairies everywhere are tired and **unhappy**, and none of them want to do anything."

"What happens if the light of the stars goes out?" Nicky asked.

A dark look crossed the prince's face. "Starlight will be lost forever."

Then Astro stopped in front of a door and opened it enough for Will and the Thea Sisters to look inside. There were **seven fairies** in the room, Astro's seven cousins.

Each of the fairies was leafing through a book, **frowning**. One of them **YAWNED**, and then all the rest of them followed.

"They've been like this for **days**," Prince Astro explained.

"What is the book they are reading?" Violet asked.

"They look through the ancient STORIES OF THE KINGDOM to remember the times when Starlight was a world full of life and joy," the prince replied. "The other fairies of the court have tried in every which way to **DISTRACT** them, but it's been no use."

"Those **poor fairies**. They look so unhappy," Violet said.

Prince Astro closed the door. "I didn't want to make you sad as well, but I needed to show you how bad the situation is."

"We will find Cometta!" Will exclaimed, determined. "You said that the four pearls of light can produce a ray of light that can find anyone or anything who is lost. Do you have a map of the kingdom?"

"I have something even better than a map," Astro answered. "Follow me."

He took them to the south wing of the castle. There was no one in the hallways there, either. The large rooms were empty and the *heavy silence* made the atmosphere somber.

The prince stopped in front of a door. He opened it and signaled to the others to enter.

"This is the royal Library," he told them.

"How marvemouse!" Violet exclaimed dreamily, looking across the ROWS and ROWS of shelves filled with books. golden ladders reached the top of the tallest shelves.

Prince Astro noticed the wonder on the faces of the **THEA SISTERS**.

"All the books that you see have been kept here since the beginning of the Starlight Kingdom," he informed them. "Some of them are super rare, and others are so ancient that they tell the story of stars that don't exist anymore."

 **Curious**, Paulina approached one of the shelves to take a closer look.

"The History and Myths of the Fairies of the Cold Stars," she read out loud. It was a **collection** of twelve books with blue velvet covers, and the titles were STAMPED in elegant silver letters.

Violet picked up one of the volumes and **delicately** caressed the cover. "Who knows how many *fascinating stories* are in these books," she remarked.

Then everyone's **ATTENTION** moved to the center of the room, which was occupied by a large bright blue globe decorated with beautiful, strange symbols. A CRYSTAL disk was set at the globe's base. Four round indents had been carved around the base — each one the size of one of the pearls of light.

"The pearls go into the base of the globe," Prince Astro instructed. He pointed to the slot marked *W* for west. "The Cosmic Forest is in the WEST so that pearl goes here."

"I get it!" Pam cried. They quickly put the rest of the pearls in the base: the pearl from the Primal Asteroid in the EAST, the pearl from the Cloudy Peaks in the NORTH, and the pearl from Lake Celeste in the SOUTH.

When all four pearls were on the base,

each one of them let out the purest *RAY OF LIGHT* and the globe began to spin around.

The rays united and the light pointed up toward a **QUARTZ STAR** on the ceiling. That light reflected onto the walls of the room, bringing forth a map of stars that couldn't be seen under regular light.

Finally, the globe stopped and the *LIGHT* pointed to an area on the map where there was a cluster of stars far away from the castle. **"That is where cometta is!"** Prince Astro exclaimed.

ASTRO AND COMETTA

Prince Astro sadly stared at the map. "Cometta is VERY FAR from here," he said.

"Do you know that place?" Will asked.

"Unfortunately, I don't, but I do know how to get there," the prince responded.

"Does that mean you're COMING with us?" Will asked.

"Yes," the prince answered.

"Then we should get moving," Colette said.

Pam groaned. "More walking? I need to get new space boots. I am wearing mine out!"

Astro smiled. "This time we won't go over any BRIDGES OF LIGHT. That would take too long."

"How will we get there?" Paulina asked.

"We will fly there," the prince replied. "I

will explain everything in a moment, but first I want to show you something."

The prince **LED** his guests out of the library, into a cozier room, where he invited them to sit on a golden silk couch. Then Astro approached a desk, opened a drawer, and took out an object that he showed to Will and the Thea Sisters.

It was a small **WATERCOLOR** painting of a young girl with a round and kind face, big happy eyes, and light-colored hair.

"This is a photo of Cometta, when she was a **CHILD**," he responded. "She and I would often play together."

"Is that why you kept her portrait?" Paulina asked.

Prince Astro smiled sadly. "It is a reminder of happier times. When Cometta became the master of harmony, everything changed."

"She doesn't live at the palace?" Violet asked.

The prince shook his head. "It is her home base, but most of the time she has to travel throughout the kingdom, checking on the **STARS** and learning new *dances* to

teach the seven fairy cousins," he explained.

"You must miss her a lot," Colette said. She could tell that the prince cared **deeply** for the fairy.

But the prince didn't seem to want to admit that. "Everyone misses her, of course," he said. "Not just me."

"Are there other portraits of Cometta? It could be useful to know what she looks like now," Will said.

"There are none, but she isn't very different

from when she was a kid in this picture," Astro replied. "Her eyes and her smile are the same as they were then, sweet and happy."

He looked up at the ceiling, as if recalling **MEMORIES**. Then he looked back down.

"Cometta has a distinctive mark as well," Astro added. "It's a STAR-SHAPED beauty mark on the inside of her left wrist."

"That will definitely **HELP** us," Will noted.

Astro stood up and walked across the room and opened up a chest. He took out a small **sword** and tucked it into his belt. "This is not a weapon of destruction. It can only do good, and I believe it will help us free Cometta. Now please follow me to the **Dragonery**," the prince instructed.

Nicky's mouth dropped open. "Dragonery? Do you mean . . . as in **dragons**?" she asked.

"Precisely," the prince replied, and he

strode with purpose down the castle hallway. "I have two **celeſtial dragonſ**. They are very tame, and very fast."

The Thea Sisters' minds **RACED** as they made their way through the castle, wondering what kind of dragons they were about to see. Prince Astro stopped in front of a large door and opened it.

Inside the room were two large dragons with **SHIMMERING** blue scales and wings the color of silver starlight. Attached to them was an ornate **golden carriage**.

"Climb aboard!" Prince Astro instructed. They did, and on his command, the dragons **flew off** into the sky.

APHELIA AND THE GIFT OF TIME

The Thea Sisters had already flown in other **fantasy** worlds before this, but the this flight was truly unique!

"This is awesome!" Nicky said. "We're flying through the stars and planets in a sky studded with hundreds of sparkly lights!"

The mice were happy on the journey, but Prince Astro was **concentrating** very hard on the route they had to take.

Finally, the carriage began to descend toward a very small purple star. It looked **DESERTED** except for one lone house.

"Is this where **Cometta** is?" Colette asked.

Astro shook his head. "No, but we can't go any farther with the information we have. I need some help with **directions**."

"And you think we will find them here?" Paulina asked.

"I know the fairy who lives on this star, and I think that she will be able to help us," the prince explained. "She is very wise."

He steered the dragons toward the house and soon the **wheels** of the carriage touched the dusty ground of the star and stopped. Astro got down, followed by the others, and walked to the entrance of the house.

"Who's there?" asked a small voice from inside.

"It is Prince Astro, Aphelia," he replied. The door opened suddenly, and an elderly fairy appeared in the doorway with a **SURPRISED LOOK** on her face.

We will ask for her help . . .

"Astro? It's always a pleasure to

see you, but I wasn't expecting a VISIT," she said.

He nodded. "I can imagine, it's been a long time since I was last in these parts."

"Let's see . . . it's been at least twelve **hourglasses**," she responded.

Will and the mouselets glanced at one another, but stayed quiet.

"Who are they?" the fairy asked, pointing to the mice.

"They are *friends*," Astro replied. "They have traveled to Starlight from far away, just to help us."

It's been so long . . .

The fairy invited them inside the house, which was full of **hourglasses** of all kinds, colors, and sizes.

"**Aphelia** is the most famous hourglass maker in the

kingdom," Astro explained. "She made her first one when she was a young fairy."

Aphelia smiled. "Oh, yes, it's a very old **PASSION** of mine," she said. "Do you know anything that is more *interesting* than time?" Aphelia asked. "Time is **ETERNAL**. It is the only thing that accompanies us from the day we are **BORN** to our last day in the stars."

"That is a very wise **THOUGHT**, fairy Aphelia," Will said.

She raised an eyebrow. "I don't think, however, that you've come here for my hourglasses, or am I **wrong**?" she asked.

"You are correct," Prince Astro said. "We need your help to find a fairy."

Prince Astro launched into the story about the disappearance of Cometta and the danger that the **STARLIGHT WORLD** was facing.

"Then these brave strangers arrived and tracked down the four pearls of light," he informed her. "They directed us to this cluster of stars. But I am not sure where to find Cometta. Have you seen her?"

"What does she look like?" Aphelia asked.

Prince Astro described her **kind** face and her silvery hair. "And she has a star-shaped beauty mark on her wrist."

The fairy's face brightened. "Oh, yes, I do remember her!"

"You mean she passed through here?" Astro asked.

"Yes, she used to pass here often, in fact," she said. "I would offer her a **cup** of tea and show her my latest hourglasses. But she has not been here in a long time."

"No one in Brightstar has had any **WORD** of her," Astro said.

"Maybe Cometta told you some **DETAIL** about her travels that could be useful for us to find her," Paulina speculated.

"Did she mention **traveling** to any of the other stars in this cluster?" Colette asked.

"Hmmm," Aphelia said, thinking. "Now that I think about it, the last time I saw her she said she was headed to a distant star at the far north end of this star cluster."

"What do you know about this star?" Will asked.

"I believe she had been there before," Aphelia said. "There is a celestial **centaur** by the name of **SIRIUS** who watches the star. Cometta said that he knew some of the oldest dances in the universe, and he was sharing them with her."

"A centaur," Prince Astro echoed. "Half fairy, half beast."

"Thank you," Paulina told Aphelia. "Now we know where to go!"

"If you plan on traveling beyond the northern borders to **REACH** the centaur's star, you must be very careful," the fairy warned. "You are dealing with dark and unexplored lands."

"I promise you we will be CAREFUL, Aphelia," Astro replied.

"I hope you find Cometta soon for her sake, and for the sake of the kingdom," the fairy responded.

Prince Astro shook her hand. "THANK YOU so much, Aphelia. You have been very helpful." Then he turned to leave.

"Wait a moment!" the fairy cried. She hurried to a cabinet in a corner of the room and opened it. She took something out of it and returned to the others.

"You strangers are **kind** to help our kingdom," she said. "Here is a *gift* for each of you."

She handed them each a pendant shaped like a tiny hourglass.

"These are a gift so you don't ever forget the importance of time," the fairy concluded. "The sand inside those bulbs is stardust, so take care of it!"

"What a **_wonderful_** gift! Thank you!" Colette said.

They all thanked Aphelia and then slipped on their pendants. Then they turned the hourglasses and watched the sand move from one bulb to the other.

"Good-bye, friend," Prince Astro said. "We must be on our way to the **FARAWAY** star of Sirius the centaur!"

THE TRAPS OF
THE CENTAUR

Prince Astro steered the golden carriage through long, empty STRETCHES of space. Occasionally they would pass a lone star twinkling, or a group of sparkly clouds.

They traveled on and on until they spotted a cold blue star hanging in the horizon.

"This is the northernmost star in the kingdom," Prince Astro said.

"Then this has to be the home of Sirius the centaur," Paulina guessed. "It doesn't look very inviting."

When they got closer, they saw that in the center of the star stood an imposing fortress made of stone, topped with towers, and surrounded by a granite labyrinth that protected the entrance.

Prince Astro commanded the two dragons to fly over the labyrinth and land on top of the castle. They moved to obey, but then they **STOPPED** suddenly.

Whomp! The dragons bounced back as though they had hit an invisible wall. The jolt nearly sent Violet flying out of the carriage.

"**Help!**" she yelled.

"I've got you!" Nicky reassured her, grabbing firmly on to her arm. At the same time, the others grabbed on to the sides of the carriage to keep from falling.

"It's an invisible shield," Prince Astro said. "I've seen them used to defend against enemy attacks, but that was many years ago. Ours is a peaceful kingdom."

"Is there a way to get past the **SHIELD**?" Nicky asked.

"Unfortunately not," the prince answered. "We must land on the star's surface and continue on foot."

"That means we must pass through the labyrinth to reach the fortress," Colette concluded.

Astro nodded. "I'm afraid so," he said. Then he called out to the dragons, "Land on the surface of the star!"

The dragons flew down and landed on the cold blue surface.

"The light is different on this star," Paulina observed immediately.

"It's a cold star," Prince Astro explained. "It takes on this blue color and doesn't make much light because of the low temperatures."

"Are there many cold stars in the kingdom?" Nicky asked.

The prince shook his head. "There are very

few," he answered. But if we do not free Cometta, many other warm and bright stars will become like this one."

"The labyrinth entrance is that way," Will said, pointing. "Let's go!"

"This labyrinth looked fairly COMPLICATED from the air," Colette commented as they stepped inside. "I hope we don't get lost."

"I thought of that when we were up there," Paulina said with a grin. "So I snapped a picture of it with my wrist computer!"

She held out the screen to show them. "I can *enlarge* it as we go. We should be able to get to the EXIT in no time."

"Smart thinking, agent!" Will said, and Paulina beamed.

"*Which way* do we go?" Pam asked.

Paulina looked at her screen. "Let's go down this way and make the first left."

They **QUICKLY** made their way through the first few turns . . . left, then right, then left, then left . . .

"This is a piece of cake!" Pam said. "Which reminds me, I sure could go for a piece of cake right about now."

Suddenly, the ground began to shake beneath their feet.

"Great globs of Gouda, the walls of the labyrinth are . . . moving!" Pam exclaimed.

Everything's moving!

"It's not possible!" Violet cried in disbelief.

Prince Astro touched one of the walls and frowned.

"It is indeed **POSSIBLE**," he said. "This is not a normal labyrinth. It's a rotating one!"

"A rotating labyrinth?" Pam repeated.

"The stone **WALLS** are set on a rotating base," the prince explained. "At timed intervals, they move one way or the other, so the Maze is constantly changing."

IN a Rotating Labyrinth, everything constantly changes!

Paulina groaned. "That means the picture I took from the sky is **USELESS**."

"I think it also means that getting through this labyrinth is IMPOSSIBLE," Pam said.

"Maybe not impossible, but it won't be easy to find Cometta," Colette said.

"We can't give up," Will said. "Let's keep moving. We will figure this out."

He walked ahead, and the others followed him.

They were all
determined
to reach the
fortress . . .

UNEXPECTED HELP

Prince Astro, Will, and the Thea Sisters made their way through the **labyrinth**, trying to get to the fortress. They made **turn** after **turn** after **turn**, but every time they got close to figuring it out, the walls moved around them. When they moved again, they would find themselves facing a **BLOCKED** wall.

After an hour of trying, Nicky gave the wall a kick.

"This is **not fair**!" she cried.

"You're right. This is the most **DISRESPECTFUL** labyrinth I've ever been stuck in," Colette complained.

"This is very **frustrating**," Will agreed. "But there has to be a way to figure this out. Let's put our heads together."

"Okay, let's think," Paulina said.

They were **quiet** for a moment.

"Hey, who's *singing*?" Pam asked. "You're breaking my concentration."

"Not me!" everyone else answered.

"Shhhh!" Prince Astro put his finger to his lips. They quieted down, and then they all heard it: the sound of a melodic voice singing.

"It's **Cometta**!" the prince exclaimed. "That's the song that we would sing when we would play in the castle's park as kids."

"She sounds close," Violet remarked.

"I think she's singing to help us figure out where she is!" Colette said.

"I believe you are **RIGHT**," the prince said. "Do as I say, and we will reach her very soon. Close your **EYES** and line up, then put a paw on the mouse in front of you. I'll go first."

"Why do we have to keep our **eyes** closed?" Colette asked.

"It's the only way to **beat** the labyrinth," Astro replied. "If we close our eyes, we will have to trust our HEARTS, and Cometta's song."

Violet nodded. "If our minds can't figure this out, our hearts will!"

They lined up as the prince suggested, and began to walk on his **signal**. Astro followed the voice of his old friend Cometta.

"Her voice is getting **LOUDER**," Nicky said hopefully.

"I believe she is close by," Astro replied. "Let's keep walking with our eyes closed and we will **REACH** her soon, I'm sure of it."

Everyone trusted Astro and his intuition, and tried not to worry about the moving walls. Suddenly, Astro stopped.

"Cometta? Are you here?" he called out.

"Astro!" a voice answered.

They all opened their eyes, and then they saw her. The fairy was IMPRISONED inside a shining sphere, but she was smiling.

"Cometta!" he cried, and he ran toward her. The Thea Sisters could see that his eyes were bright with emotion. He placed his hand against the sphere.

"Astro, it's really you!" Cometta said.

"I am so happy to have finally found you! I was so **WORRIED** about you!" he said happily.

"How did you figure out where I was? I had almost lost all hope," she responded.

"It's a long story, but I couldn't have done it without these kind mice, whom I now call my friends," Astro explained, pointing to the Thea Sisters and Will.

Astro, it's you!

I will free you!

"THANK YOU with all my heart," the fairy said to them.

"We are happy to help," Will responded. "But now we need to find a way to FREE you!"

At Will's words, Astro took the sword out of his belt. When he held it next to the **sphere** that was holding Cometta prisoner, the sword began to glow.

"This sword was **forged** in the Silver Goblins' furnace," the prince said. "It was made of a magical precious metal capable of breaking all chains and evil spells."

"Will it be **dangerous** for Cometta?" Paulina asked.

"I have full trust in Prince Astro," Cometta replied confidently.

The two looked each other in the eyes for the LONGEST time, and then Cometta nodded without speaking. Astro approached the sphere, lifted his sword, and gave it a sharp **BLOW**.

The sphere split in two and **EXPLODED** in a cloud of silver dust that scattered in the sky.

"**I'm free!**" the fairy exclaimed.

Cometta reached out to make sure that the sphere had truly disappeared, and then she ran toward Astro. The prince embraced her as the others looked on, touched by the sweet scene.

"THANK YOU, Astro," she said. "I didn't think I would ever get out."

"I was willing to do whatever it took to **save you**, Cometta. Starlight needs you, and I do, too," he replied.

"**HOW ROMANTIC!**" Violet commented to her friends under her breath.

"Those two must be in love," Colette agreed.

"Even if they don't know it yet," Paulina added with a smile.

"Well, I'm pretty sure they'll figure it out real soon," Violet concluded.

Astro became serious. "Did Sirius the centaur imprison you?" he asked Cometta.

The fairy nodded.

"I promise that he will pay for what he has done," the prince assured her.

"But why did he behave that way? Did he want to **DESTROY** his own kingdom?" Will asked.

"It's not what you think," Cometta said. "Sirius needs our *help*. Let me explain."

A MYSTERIOUS
AMULET

"I know that you have formed a very bad **opinion** of Sirius," Cometta began. "But things are not what they seem."

"He **TRAPPED** you in that sphere, right?" Pam asked.

"That is true," Cometta replied. "But **SIRIUS** isn't evil. I say that because I've known him for a long time. He has always been an honest and valiant **knight**. Or at least, he was until recently."

"What do you mean?" Astro asked.

"During my last trip here, before he **imprisoned** me in the sphere, I noticed that something had changed in him," Cometta remembered. "He said he wanted to erase the harmony of our world. He wanted to **turn out** the light of the stars and give the kingdom over to darkness forever."

"I'm sorry, but anyone who says something like that has to be **EVIL**," Nicky said. "So why are you so sure that he isn't?"

"Because I had known Sirius for so long, I couldn't believe that he had changed so much," the fairy continued. "I stayed and OBSERVED him, trying to find out what was wrong. And that was when I noticed it."

"Noticed what?" Pam asked.

"Around his neck he wore a **strange amulet**," she answered. "I realized that I had never seen it before."

"What does it look like?" Prince Astro asked.

"It is a **SEVEN-POINTED** star made of dark metal," Cometta replied.

Astro's eyes widened in astonishment. "Before I took the throne, my parents told me of a very powerful amulet with **EVIL POWERS** that they had buried in a secret place so that no one could use it to cause harm. They showed me a picture of it: a dark star with seven points."

"It could be the same amulet," Cometta guessed. "Sirius had found it during one of his travels beyond the borders of the kingdom."

"That might explain the change in his behavior," Paulina said. "The **EVIL POWERS** of the star could be corrupting his spirit."

Cometta nodded. "That is what I thought, too. His behavior is not **NATURAL**. I believe the amulet is causing it."

"We need to take that amulet from him," Paulina said.

Will nodded. "Exactly. And we must. act quickly. Once he realizes that we have freed Cometta, he will try to stop us. And he is **DANGEROUS** as long as he wears the amulet."

"We must attack him without warning!" Prince Astro cried.

Cometta placed a hand on the prince's arm. "I think we can save Sirius without **fighting** him. He had no idea of the amulet's dark powers when he got it. It's holding him PRISONER, and we must free him from its spell."

"Fine," Prince Astro said. "But if he tries to **HARM** any of you, he will have to face me!"

"Follow me," Cometta said, and she led them through the labyrinth.

"It has stopped moving," Violet observed.

"The amulet's magic also controlled the moving walls," Cometta explained. "I think when Astro **DESTROYED** the sphere, he broke the magic's hold on the labyrinth."

"I'm curious — how did you know that your **song** would safely lead us to you?" Colette asked the fairy.

"Music is the best way to reawaken ties of the heart," Cometta answered. "And MEMORIES are stronger than any evil spell."

She led them around a corner of the maze to a row that opened up right in front of the door of the castle.

"Finally!" Pam cheered.

Then they heard the sound of HOOVES, and the front door opened to reveal a man with the legs of a horse and the upper body of a FAIRY.

IT WAS SIRIUS!

The centaur let out a **chilling** cry and reared up on his hind legs.

"How dare you FREE my prisoner?" he thundered.

Astro stepped forward. "I am Astro, the prince of Starlight. You had no right to IMPRISON Cometta!"

"You are too far from your *beautiful* castle to give

I challenge you!

What?!

orders," Sirius replied **arrogantly**. "I challenge you to an archery contest. If you win, you are free. If you lose, you will be my prisoners forever."

"Shouldn't we **tackle** him and get the amulet?" Nicky whispered.

"That could be **DANGEROUS**," Will whispered back. "Prince Astro will know what to do."

"Those are arrows that are magically powered with galaxy winds," Astro said. "They are extremely challenging to shoot and aim."

"Yes, and I happen to be an expert in shooting them," Sirius informed them.

The prince nodded.

"We will accept your challenge, Sirius," Cometta told him. "But if you lose, you must give us the *star pendant* you wear."

His hand flew to the amulet, which let off a sinister sparkle.

"No, this is mine," he objected.

"Are you afraid of **LOSING**, then?" the fairy challenged him.

"Of course not!" he protested.

Colette joined in. "I thought you told us that Sirius was **BRAVE**. But I guess not."

"I used to think so, but I am not sure anymore," Cometta added.

"I am not afraid to lose! Let the challenge begin!" he thundered.

Cometta smiled at Colette. Taunting the centaur had worked.

THE COMPETITION COULD BEGIN!

THE CENTAUR'S CHALLENGE

"We get **three shots** each," Sirius explained as he led them to the castle's archery range. "A point will be given for each arrow that hits the bull's-eye."

Nicky approached Prince Astro. "I would like to try, too, Prince," she proposed. "I am an experienced archer."

Prince Astro nodded. "Good," he said. "We can take turns shooting. This might give us more of a *chance*."

Listening to his two opponents, Sirius chuckled. "So it will take two of you to *BEAT* me, will it? Fine," he said. "I'll go first."

Sirius grabbed the bow and loaded it with an **arrow** with a tip that looked like a tiny, **spiraling** cyclone.

He pulled it back, aimed it, and let it go. The arrow darted like **lightning**, pulled by the wind tip into twists and turns. It changed direction **again** and **again** as it headed for the target. For a moment, it looked like he would **miss** the bull's-eye.

But after all those turns, the arrow landed smack in the center of it!

I'll start!

"One **point** for me," Sirius said, clearly satisfied. Then he passed the bow and arrow to the prince.

Astro carefully nocked the arrow, aimed it, took a deep breath, and **CONCENTRATED** with all his might. When he felt ready, he let the string of the **BOW** go and watched and followed the zigzag path of the arrow. Like the one that Sirius shot, his made various twists in the air before landing in the very center of the **bull's-eye**.

"I am in awe, Prince," said the centaur with a **SARCASTIC** smile. "Don't get your hopes up," he added. "No one beats me with a bow and arrow. Watch me take this second shot and you will see who really is the *best*!"

Sirius, once again, got in position and aimed his arrow. And once more the arrow **SHOT** right into the center of the target.

"Another point for me!" Sirius announced. Then he smirked at Nicky. "Your turn, YOUNG ONE."

Nicky looked at the prince. "How were you able to control your arrow?"

"Shooting a galaxy arrow requires a mix of skill and heart," Prince Astro replied. "First, make sure your aim is true. Then have faith that it will hit the target."

Nicky nodded. "Got it," she said confidently, and she took the bow and an arrow from Sirius.

She got into STRIKING POSITION and

then closed her eyes, remembering how much fun it was to shoot a bow and arrow on her ranch in Australia.

There, her family and friends would cheer for her, filling her with confidence and CALM. This was a very different situation, with the fate of a FANTASY WORLD at stake.

I can do it . . .

She felt the scornful gaze of the centaur on her, and froze for a moment. Then she took a deep breath and gazed at the Thea Sisters. They always gave her the strength she needed.

"Skill and heart," she muttered under her breath. She nocked the arrow, aiming it directly for the bull's-eye.

I have faith that it will hit the bull's-eye! she told herself. *You can do it, Nicky! You are a Thea Sister, and we can do anything!*

She released the arrow and watched it soar across the range. It TWISTED and turned, but it moved *faster* than either arrow shot by the prince or the centaur.

WHOOSH! It split the arrow that Sirius had shot right in two — a pure bull's-eye!

"You did it. Well done, Nicky!" Colette cheered.

Sirius snorted. "Lucky shot," he said, yanking both arrows out of the target. He took the bow from Nicky and nocked his third arrow. The amulet around his neck had become even darker, and seemed to be **beating** with energy.

Sirius pulled the bow and quickly shot the arrow, which once again hit the center of the target. Then he walked away in silence without celebrating.

"It looks like he wants this game to be **OVER**," Paulina whispered to Violet.

There was only one shot left in the challenge. Prince Astro loaded an arrow into the bow and eyed the target.

"You'll **NEVER** be able to save your kingdom. You don't have what it takes," Sirius **taunted** him, just as Astro released the arrow.

Everyone watched, holding their breath as the arrow ~~twisted~~ through the air. It neared the target — and then passed right by, missing it.

Oh no! Nicky thought. *He must have lost faith!*

"Ha!" Sirius laughed **wickedly**. "I warned

you. It was a big **MISTAKE** for you to come here. And now it is your last mistake, because all of you will be my prisoners, here . . . **forever**!"

"Or maybe you could just let us go?" Pam suggested. "We can leave right now, and we'll **FORGET** all of this happened."

The centaur only laughed.

Speechless, everyone turned to Prince Astro. Surely he had some plan? But the prince only stared at the centaur with a **MYSTERIOUS** look on his face.

"You have lost," Sirius said. "And now you will witness the power of the amulet."

He grabbed the **AMULET** and held it away from his body. "Amulet, create a dark, dreary cell that is impossible to escape!"

The amulet filled with **DARK ENERGY** as it began to cast the spell.

Then they all heard a **whoosh**. The arrow that Prince Astro had shot had CIRCLED around the target and was now heading for Sirius!

Wham! The arrow hit the amulet that Sirius had in his hand. The dark star shattered into *a thousand pieces* . . .

Then a violent **GUST** of space wind hit the centaur, throwing him to the floor.

My amulet! No!

THE POWER OF LOVE

Cometta and the mouselets watched, **stunned**, and turned toward Astro.

"What happened?" Pam asked.

"I think I know," Nicky responded. "You told me to have FAITH that your arrow would hit the target. And in your mind, you were aiming for the amulet, right?"

Prince Astro smiled. "Exactly, Nicky!" he said. "I knew that even if he had won, Sirius would find some other excuse to keep us prisoner. Until his heart was free of the amulet, we wouldn't be free, either."

"That was very SMART, Astro," Cometta told him. "Now let me make sure that Sirius is all right!"

She hurried to the centaur, who was lying on the ground, motionless, with his eyes closed.

"What happened to Sirius? Why isn't he waking up?" Violet asked.

"Maybe he's another VICTIM of the evil power of the amulet," Colette said sadly.

"There is still a piece of the amulet on the chain," Cometta noticed. "I think I know what to do, but I will need your HELP, Astro."

"Anything," the prince said, and he stood by her.

Together, they reached down and took the chain off the centaur's neck. The scattered pieces of the amulet MAGICALLY came back together.

"Uh-oh," Pam said. "That's a bad thing, right?"

"We are stronger than the DARK POWERS of this amulet," Cometta said, holding it out to Astro. He placed his hands over hers, and the amulet began to shimmer with a soft red light.

We will defeat the evil!

The others **SHIELDED** their eyes as the red light got **BRIGHTER** and **BRIGHTER**. Finally, it began to dim.

When the light FADED, the dark star in their hands had transformed into a beautiful **GOLD STAR** that pulsed with warm positive light.

"It looks like all the dark magic is gone," Paulina said. "But how did that happen?"

"We **TRANSFORMED** the amulet," Cometta replied.

"How is that *possible*?" Nicky asked.

"I might have an idea," Colette whispered, nodding toward Astro and Cometta.

The two fairies were **gazing** into each

other's eyes and **SMILING** tenderly.

"Oh, I get it," Pam said. "They're in **love**!"

"And the **power** of their love must have overcome the dark energy in the amulet, transforming it into GOOD energy," Paulina guessed.

"The power of love always **wins** in the end!" Colette added.

Finally freed from the amulet, Sirius opened his eyes a few moments later and slowly sat up. Disoriented, he looked around.

"What happened to me?" he asked.

"You were the victim of a SPELL," Astro replied.

"Prince Astro! You're here?" the centaur asked in SURPRISE, and he immediately **bowed** his head to show respect for the ruler of Starlight.

"It's a long story, Sirius," the prince told

him. "But luckily, it has a happy ending." He smiled Sweetly at Cometta.

"How do you feel now?" the fairy asked the centaur.

"A bit confused, to tell the truth," he responded. Then he continued to stare at Cometta and some memories came back to him. "You . . . you were in my labyrinth . . . imprisoned! Did I lock you in that sphere?" he asked.

The fairy nodded. "Yes, but it wasn't your fault."

"Then why did I behave in such a HORRIBLE way?" he asked.

Prince Astro!

How are you, Sirius?

"Because of this," the fairy explained, showing him the star. "It was an **EVIL** amulet, but now it has TRANSFORMED into a source of positive energy."

"Do you **REMEMBER** how you got it?" the prince asked him.

The centaur concentrated as if he was recalling a distant memory. Then he nodded.

"My job is to **GUARD** this star and the cosmic space at the extreme northern ends of the kingdom," he began. "One day, on a small deserted star, I **FOUND** this strange amulet. It was almost entirely buried in red sand, but its sparkles got my attention. Filled with curiosity, I picked it up. As soon as I had it in my hands, I felt the need to put it around my neck, and so I did. From that moment, though, my **memories** are a bit confused."

"You no longer have to worry about the

amulet," the prince reassured him.

Sirius bowed again. "Thank you, Prince Astro. And thank you, Cometta. I am deeply sorry for what I have done."

"It's all in the past," the fairy answered.

"You had no control over your actions, Sirius," Prince Astro said. "I am certain that you were a loyal and courageous knight, and you will be again.

"**HURRAY!**" the Thea Sisters cheered.

"We couldn't have asked for a better ending to this story," Colette remarked.

"Well, I could think of **one thing** that would make it even better," Pam said.

"Don't say it," Nicky warned.

Pam turned to the centaur. "You wouldn't happen to have any PIZZA in this castle, would you?"

A CELEBRATORY RETURN

It was as if a cloud of darkness had been lifted from the star. Sirius was **free** from the evil power of the amulet. Cometta was free from her prison, and she was reunited with her BELOVED Prince Astro.

"We should get back to BRIGHTSTAR," Will said. "Cometta is needed to save the kingdom."

"Of course!" Cometta said. "But before I leave . . ."

She approached Sirius and gave him the **STAR-SHAPED** pendant.

"This is for you," she told him.

He looked surprised. "Why do you want to give it to me?"

"Because the light is positive now, and it is

You keep it!

Thank you!

so **STRONG** that it can be seen throughout the kingdom. If you need us, shine the light and we will see it," she answered.

"It is a precious gift, and I will treasure it. Thank you," the centaur replied.

He led them outside the castle, back to the GOLDEN CARRIAGE. The prince, Cometta, and the mice climbed on board. Astro grabbed the dragons' reins.

"GOOD-bye, SiRius!" the Thea Sisters called out.

"**SEE YOU SOON!**" Astro added. At his signal, the dragons took off and the carriage lifted up in the air toward the luminous star-filled sky.

"You were right to give Sirius the pendant," the prince said to Cometta.

"I wanted him to have a **KEEPSAKE** that

We're going home!

Good-bye, Sirius!

would help him feel like a part of our marvelous starry world," she told him.

"You truly have a big heart, Cometta," the prince told her.

"You inspire the **best** part of me," she said with a smile.

The Thea Sisters listened to them talk.

"I can see why Cometta's job is to bring harmony to the kingdom," Violet remarked. "She has a very positive spirit."

"And now that she can return to her role, all of the Starlight world will go back to shining brightly," Colette added.

Paulina gazed out at the twinkling stars they passed in the carriage. "Everything seems BRIGHTER already."

"It's true! Even if the seven cousins haven't begun to dance, something has changed," Colette agreed.

"And it is thanks to you, agents. I am very PROUD of you," Will said. "This was no easy mission, but you faced it **BRAVELY**."

"Thank you, Will," Violet said. "We couldn't do it without you leading us!"

"That's for sure," Pam agreed.

"Hey, look!" Nicky cried out. "Is that BRIGHTSTAR in the distance?"

They followed her gaze to the sparkling towers of Brightstar Castle, poking out like a precious gem at the top of a white rock. The Silver Stairway sparkled beneath them.

"Wow! What a marvemouse sight!" Nicky exclaimed.

"I can't wait to see what it looks like when its brightness is restored," Violet remarked.

Prince Astro landed the carriage outside the Dragonery, and they all climbed out.

Cometta looked around at the castle,

smiling. "How nice to be back. It's as though I've been gone **forever**," she remarked wistfully.

"You can stay at the palace for as **LONG** as you want," Astro said, adding, "My seven fairy cousins will be very happy to see you again."

"Let's go find them," Cometta suggested.

Astro led them to the great hall, and then

Cometta! How wonderful to see you!

I'm so happy! You've come back!

opened the door. The seven cousins looked up, and as soon as they saw Cometta, they ran to meet her.

"I am so happy to be back!" Cometta said. "Are you ready for a new star DANCE?"

"Of course! We are more than ready!" the seven cousins responded.

Cometta danced a few steps, and the others copied her. As they danced, a light shone from them. They floated up off the floor, still dancing, and the light swirled around them. It RADIATED out through the room, into the castle, and outside into the world of Starlight.

"I think the time has come to celebrate our newfound harmony," Prince Astro announced. "This is the perfect occasion to invite all the inhabitants of the kingdom to a star dance!"

THE GREAT
STAR DANCE

Excitement filled Brightstar Castle as everyone got excited for the big event.

THE *Great Star Dance*

Astro and Cometta had organized the **party** with the help of the prince's seven cousins and the entire fairy court. The **invitations** were written by hand on elegant star paper and sent to everyone in the kingdom. The rooms of the castle were decorated with strings of light, ribbons, and flowers, in a triumph of colors and **shiny** sparkles.

Music played throughout the halls as the fairies **flitted** around, infusing everything with joy and PURE HARMONY.

Will and the Thea Sisters walked around the castle, watching the preparations. Each room they entered was more *beautiful* than the last and held new surprises.

"The atmosphere of this dance is truly MAGICAL," Paulina remarked.

"It's too bad we don't have anything magical to wear," Colette said with a sigh.

"Maybe we could put some of the decorations in our hair," Violet proposed.

That moment, Cometta approached the five friends.

"There you are!" she said. "The fairies have made five dresses just for you to thank you for what you've done for Starlight," she told them. "Let me take you to the court's tailor for a fitting."

"We would love that!" Colette replied eagerly.

Cometta led them into a dressing room with mirrored doors where the fairies of the court were waiting for them.

"These are for you," one of the fairies said, showing them the dresses. "We hope you like them. We made them based on your nature and personalities!"

"They are marvemouse!" Colette exclaimed, her eyes sparkling with happiness.

Cometta smiled and invited the mouselet to try on the dress the fairies had made for her.

"You are beautiful!" the other Thea Sisters commented in awe.

"It truly is perfect for you," Cometta agreed.

Everyone else tried on their dresses. Even though they were all different, they had a common charm: They were sparkly and **MYSTERIOUS** just like the Starlight world.

"You all look like star fairies!" Cometta

A Starry ... Evening!

For the Great Star Dance, the fairies gave the mouselets these dreamy dresses to wear! Here they are!

Colette

A floor-length dress made with the finest pink silk, with a light cape, and a silver belt. The sandals and earrings are the purest moon crystal.

Nicky

A long emerald green dress adorned with drops of light. Completing the outfit are a cloak with flared sleeves, a matching headband, and star-shaped earrings.

PAULINA

An elegant dress with long sleeves adorned with pieces of sparkling meteorite. Drop earrings and a belt with a star adornment finish the look.

PAMELA

A sleeveless red satin jumpsuit with a shooting-star train. Her sandals and jewelry are adorned with moonstone.

Violet

A lilac dress with a full skirt and violet sparkles. Her hair is pulled back to highlight the earrings made with small precious fragments of celestial rock.

commented when they were all dressed.

Paulina smiled. "You could not have given us a nicer compliment," she replied.

"What dress will you wear?" Colette asked.

"Actually, it's a surprise for me, too!" the fairy replied. "Astro's seven cousins made it and sewed it, and now I'm going to go and see it for the first time."

"I can't wait to see it!" Violet said. "It's got to be something special."

Cometta left the room. Colette turned to the others.

"I have a funny feeling that there are some great surprises in store here tonight," she said.

"Coco, your **INTUITION** is never wrong," Paulina said. "If you *think* something is going to happen, I am sure it will."

Colette, in fact, was not wrong . . .

Wearing their new dresses, the Thea Sisters made their way to the palace BALLROOM, where they met Will. The fairies had made a new suit for him that seemed to SHIMMER.

The other guests had already arrived, and they were wearing incredible outfits, too.

"Everything is so beautiful!" Colette exclaimed, enchanted. "These decorations sparkle as if . . . as if . . ."

"As if they were stars!" Nicky said, finishing her sentence.

"They are!" exclaimed a fairy who was passing by. "They are star lights, the smallest stars in all the kingdom. We collected them for this special occasion. When the PARTY is over, you just blow them in the wind to scatter them in the sky."

"That's amazing," Colette said. "We should try to bring some back to decorate our dorm room, right, Pam? Pam . . . ?"

She turned to see her friend holding a plate filled with tiny desserts.

"Pam, we just got here!" Colette scolded.

"How am I supposed to resist these **delicacies**?" Pam asked. "The glimmer fairies made them."

Then a hush fell over the room, and the crowd of guests parted as Cometta made her entrance. She was dressed in a beautiful pearl-colored gown decorated with **golden** embroidery.

Astro crossed the room and met her in the center. Then he knelt in front of her. He looked up, gazing into her eyes.

"Cometta, when we were apart, I realized that there is a deep connection between us," he said. "Now that I have found you again, I know that I want to spend my life with you.

Would you do me the HONOR of becoming my wife?"

Cometta's eyes lit up. "Yes, my beloved PRINCE!" she answered.

Everyone applauded as Astro put on her head a star-shaped crown embedded with real, tiny stars: the *Star Crown*.

"Three cheers for the **royal couple**!" someone yelled, and the room exploded with joy, singing, and dancing that lasted all night.

We will be married!

TiME TO GO HOME

The next day, the Thea Sisters and Will met Astro and Cometta in the throne room.

"Prince Astro, Cometta, unfortunately the **MOMENT** has come for us to go home," Will explained.

Thanks for everything!

"What a shame, but will you **come back** soon?" the fairy asked.

"We really hope so!" the Thea Sisters all answered at once.

"ALLOW ME once more to thank you for all that you've done for us and the entire Starlight Kingdom," Astro said.

"It was a pleasure, Prince," Will responded.

Cometta hugged the mouselets one by one and thanked them again. Then Will led them outside the castle where the carriage with the celestial dragons was waiting to take them to the CRYSTAL ELEVATOR.

"I'm a little sad to leave here," Violet said.

"Me, too," Colette agreed. "But we will always have our memories of this place!"

They climbed aboard, and a moment later, the carriage was soaring through the INFINITE SPACE of the kingdom of the star fairies, as the passengers said their last good-byes to the SPARKLY sky of Starlight and all its marvels.

When they got back to the SEVEN ROSES UNIT, they changed out of their space suits. Will met them at the HELICOPTER pad as they got ready for their return trip to Whale Island.

"Well done, agents!" he congratulated them. "You have carried out this mission excellently. The whole department is talking about your SUCCESS."

"We are glad. Thanks, Will!" Paulina replied.

"Until our next mission!" Pam said. "We're always ready!"

The Thea Sisters returned to Mouseford Academy at night, just in time to watch the shooting star display. They sat outside in the academy's garden, silently watching the night sky. Thoughts of the *incredible adventure* they had just had in the kingdom of the star fairies danced through their heads.

Then Paulina interrupted the silence. "Look!" she cried, pointing at the sky.

A shooting star **STREAKED** across the dark sky, leaving a faint trail of light behind it.

"Let's make a WISH, quick!" Violet proposed.

The Thea Sisters held paws and silently made wishes they held in their hearts. For a moment, they could feel the harmony of the star fairy dance, led by Cometta — and they knew they were part of it, too.

Don't miss any of my adventures in the Kingdom of Fantasy!

THE KINGDOM OF FANTASY

THE QUEST FOR PARADISE:
THE RETURN TO THE KINGDOM OF FANTASY

THE AMAZING VOYAGE:
THE THIRD ADVENTURE IN THE KINGDOM OF FANTASY

THE DRAGON PROPHECY:
THE FOURTH ADVENTURE IN THE KINGDOM OF FANTASY

THE VOLCANO OF FIRE:
THE FIFTH ADVENTURE IN THE KINGDOM OF FANTASY

THE SEARCH FOR TREASURE:
THE SIXTH ADVENTURE IN THE KINGDOM OF FANTASY

THE ENCHANTED CHARMS:
THE SEVENTH ADVENTURE IN THE KINGDOM OF FANTASY

THE PHOENIX OF DESTINY:
AN EPIC KINGDOM OF FANTASY ADVENTURE

THE HOUR OF MAGIC:
THE EIGHTH ADVENTURE IN THE KINGDOM OF FANTASY

THE WIZARD'S WAND:
THE NINTH ADVENTURE IN THE KINGDOM OF FANTASY

THE SHIP OF SECRETS:
THE TENTH ADVENTURE IN THE KINGDOM OF FANTASY

THE DRAGON OF FORTUNE:
AN EPIC KINGDOM OF FANTASY ADVENTURE

THE GUARDIAN OF THE REALM:
THE ELEVENTH ADVENTURE IN THE KINGDOM OF FANTASY

THE ISLAND OF DRAGONS:
THE TWELFTH ADVENTURE IN THE KINGDOM OF FANTASY